Little Darlings

BY

SAM LLEWELLYN

razOr
bill

Little Darlings

RAZORBILL

Published by the Penguin Group
Penguin Young Readers Group
345 Hudson Street, New York, New York 10014, U.S.A.
Penguin Group (USA) Inc., 375 Hudson Street, New York, New York 10014, U.S.A.
Penguin Books Canada Ltd, 10 Alcorn Avenue, Toronto, Ontario, Canada M4V 3B2
(a division of Pearson Penguin Canada, Inc.)
Penguin Books Ltd, 80 Strand, London WC2R 0RL, England
Penguin Ireland, 25 St Stephen's Green, Dublin 2, Ireland
(a division of Penguin Books Ltd)
Penguin Group (Australia), 250 Camberwell Road, Camberwell, Victoria 3124, Australia
(a division of Pearson Australia Group Pty Ltd)
Penguin Books India Pvt Ltd, 11 Community Centre, Panchsheel Park,
New Delhi – 110 017, India
Penguin Group (NZ), Cnr Airborne and Rosedale Roads, Albany, Auckland 1310,
New Zealand (a division of Pearson New Zealand Ltd)
Penguin Books (South Africa) (Pty) Ltd, 24 Sturdee Avenue, Rosebank,
Johannesburg 2196, South Africa

Penguin Books Ltd, Registered Offices: 80 Strand, London WC2R 0RL, England

10 9 8 7 6 5 4 3 2 1

Copyright 2004 © Sam Llewellyn
All rights reserved

Library of Congress Cataloging-in-Publication Data is available

Printed in the United States of America

In *the* splendid front hall of Number One, Avenue Marshal Posh, Nanny Dodgson unbuttoned the starched cuffs of her uniform blouse and rolled up her sleeves.

From the first landing of the great oval staircase came the whine of a hair dryer. Signor Tesiwesi, Mrs. Darling's award-winning hairdresser, was tonging away at Mrs. Darling's sticky blond beehive. As usual, Papa and Mrs. Darling were going Out to Dinner.

From a huge doorway off the marble-floored hall came the bark and grunt of Papa Darling, president and chairman of Darling Gigantic, PLC, giving instructions for the building of another office block on another nature reserve.

From upstairs on the nursery floor, where the little Darlings were held captive, came a deep, deep silence.

Nanny Dodgson finished her sleeve rolling with the neat tuck she had learned at the Royal and Ancient Academy of Nannies. Her chin was square. Her eyes gleamed calmly beneath the brim of her brown bowler hat. But under the snow white starch of her apron a flock of butterflies swooped and trembled. It was quiet. It was too quiet. Nanny Dodgson did not like it. She did not like it at all.

But this was what she had been trained for.

Taking a deep breath, she placed one shining brogue on the first of the stairs and started to climb, muttering under her breath comforting words: *Children should be seen and not heard; the devil finds work for idle hands; mind your p's and q's; patience is a virtue; virtue is a grace; Grace is a little girl who wouldn't wash her—*

"Nanny," said a thin, refined voice. Nanny Dodgson realized that her Good Thoughts had got her as far as the first landing. She stood smiling nicely, hands folded, waiting for orders. "Yes, Mrs. Darling?"

"We'll be out tonight," trilled Mrs. Darling, Signor Tesiwesi tunneling away in her hair. "Will you be all right with the children?"

"Sottinly, madam, lovely little people."

Mrs. Darling's lipsticky smile froze a little. It was such a trial when one was simply rushed off one's feet with dinner parties, and of course poor Colin had to do business at all hours and sometimes in the Bahamas. People really had no idea of the *stress* involved in bringing up children, particularly someone else's. . . .

Which reminded her of something she had been meaning to ask for days. "Nanny," she said, "how old would you say they are now?"

"Who, madam?"

"The children."

"Daisy, the eldest—"

"I always did say she was the eldest," said Mrs. Darling, nodding. She prided herself on being in touch.

"*Porca miseria,* keepa still da head," hissed Signor Tesiwesi.

"—is twelve and a half on Tuesday, naughty lumpkin," said Nanny Dodgson. "Cassian is eleven and a quarter on Wednesday next, the wee caution."

"We'll be at Lady Mortdarthur's," said Mrs. Darling. "They've been in Mustique, you know."

"Cassian is the mechanical type," said Nanny Dodgson, sniffing. "And Primrose is ten, lovaduckles ickle. Her birthday was two weeks ago. You were at the Teagardens'—"

"No, the de Barpas'," said Mrs. Darling. "Such flowers! And tell me, are the children at home?"

"Yes, madam."

"How lovely. Oh, I must dash."

"Not before is feenish the head," said Signor Tesiwesi.

Nanny Dodgson trudged on toward the silence upstairs.

If she had not been a nanny, she could have sworn that she smelled smoke.

But nannies never swear.

Three children sat in front of the nursery fire. The mantelpiece was made of Italian marble. The coal in the fireplace came from the finest seam in the country. The fork on which they were toasting a neatly trussed city pigeon was made of gold and platinum.

The walls were covered with pictures of sweet children by Renoir and teeny dolls' clothes in gilt frames, each with a label: Yves Saint Laurent, Hardy Amies, Balenciaga. Among these sweet works of art were polished mahogany shields bearing the heads of nursery mice, trapped by Cassian after complaints from Daisy and stuffed by Primrose. Among the little shields was a bigger shield, bearing a roundish, brownish object, made of threadbare plush. The brass plate under it read THE ROYAL EDWARD—PART. Under the plate, a bad child (there was no other kind in the nursery) had carved in neat capital letters: BEAR'S BUM. And indeed, dear reader, a bear's bum it was; the bum of the rarest, most priceless, most squabbled-over bear in the world.

But we are getting ahead of ourselves. One thing at a time. Are you sitting comfortably?

Well.

High on the nursery wall, a tiny bell tinkled.

"Here she comes," said Daisy. Daisy had freckles, thoughtful eyes of acid green, and splendid bloodred fingernails, which she was drying in the heat of the fire.

"Come on, Nanny, make my day," said Primrose out of the side of her mouth. Primrose had straight blond hair, an Alice hair band, and mild blue eyes, which were squinting at the faintly sizzling pigeon. Primrose was a keen and skillful cook.

"Engaging circuits one and two," said Cassian, a stocky boy with black hair that grew low over an oil-stained forehead. It made him look as if he were frowning with concentration, which in fact he usually was. "Ready? Three, two, one. Go."

How very shocking! thought Nanny Dodgson when she saw the toy car on the landing. She had been in the Darling household eighteen days precisely, and she was not yet having the effect she could have wished for. The parents were all a nanny could desire, of course—no interference there. A papa who was a busy man whose time was not his own. A mummy who was, well, not the actual mummy. More like the papa's secretary, who had spent more time with the papa than the mummy, until the mummy had been sent away and the secretary mummy had come instead. And, of course, the Mrs.

Secretary mummy knew what was best for the children, namely a nanny, strict but fair.

Ooh, yes, thought Nanny Dodgson, with the pea-sized brain in the thirty-centimeter-thick skull under the reinforced brown bowler. This was just about a perfect billet. No interference here.

Though the children were difficult, no question. For instance, thought Nanny, the toy car on the top stair. What nicely brought up child would leave a toy lying about after Nanny had told it to put its things away? Really, it was too much!

Nanny stooped to pick up the car, wheezing slightly. She was a stout, busty, solid woman, an excellent shape for a nanny but not so good for climbing stairs.

Perhaps that is why she did not see the wires that ran from the toy car, under the Turkish carpet, and through a hole hidden by the elaborate carving on the nursery door.

Nanny's fingers closed on the car. Two hundred and forty volts of electricity shot through her body. Her brown bowler whizzed off her head and lodged in the ceiling. Her iron gray hair stood clean on end, and she fizzed like a bottle of Papa Darling's Bollinger, which is, of course, a kind of champagne, astonishingly fizzy and amazingly expensive.

The car dropped from her smoking fingers. She put out her hand for the nursery door handle. Then, remembering what had happened last time she had touched something made of metal in this house, she changed her mind. Crying,

"I am coming in, wicked children!" she charged the door with her shoulder.

Reader, you may say that nannies do not charge doors like rugby forwards. Reader, you are wrong, and on this fateful evening Daisy knew better than you. "Now," she murmured, blowing on a bloodred nail.

Cassian opened the door. "Good evening, Nana," chorused the children politely.

And in came Nanny Dodgson, sideways, at forty miles an hour. She bounced off the back of the nursery sofa, was flung sharp right, and hurtled toward the door of the nursery bathroom, which Primrose opened for her.

Nanny Dodgson now seemed to be skating. She had one thought, and it was this. She could definitely smell burning. Then the time for thinking was over, because the world had turned yellow.

Yellow?

The Darling children stood in the bathroom doorway. They nodded with quiet satisfaction as Nanny Dodgson's thick brown brogues shot her across the well-soaped floor toward the bath. They shook hands gravely as she tripped and crashed into the tub, throwing up a mighty sheet of custard.

Custard?

The Darling children knew what they liked, and it was not custard, particularly when burnt. It had been one of the first things they had told Nanny Dodgson. So for the next fortnight, Nanny Dodgson had fed them burnt custard for breakfast, lunch, tea, and supper, not letting them leave the table till they had eaten it All Up.

"Do you think she'll drown?" said Daisy, who was interested in consequences.

"We'll see," said Cassian, using a phrase much employed by Darling nannies (there had been eighteen of them so far).

"She'll boil before she drowns," said Primrose, who had been responsible for lighting the small fire of logs smoldering underneath the bath. "Oops! Scatter!"

For Nanny Dodgson was rising in the bath, swathed in a daffodil veil of custard. She made a bubbling noise, in which was dimly audible a drizzle of nanny talk: "Never in all my born days . . . Your poor parents . . . It will never do. . . . Go to bed without your suppers." The custard mountain stepped out of the bath and blobbed yellowly out of the door.

"Phase three," said Cassian, taking up the slack on a small winch.

Nanny Dodgson squelched toward the top of the stairs. She was seeing red, mixed with yellow.

What she was not seeing were trip wires.

Her brogue caught Cassian's ingenious contrivance. She plummeted down the stairs like a custard pinwheel.

Mrs. Darling put the finishing touches to her forehead polish, fluffed up the tulle flounces of her bodice, and blew herself a sticky scarlet kiss in the huge gilt mirror. Lady Mortdarthur would be green about her hair. Signor Tesiwesi had done such a divine job—

But what was all this noise?

She stepped out onto the landing. Sixteen stone of Dodgson knocked her flat. Tangled together, Mrs. Darling and Nanny descended to the hall like a bulk delivery of custard. They lay under the chandelier, moaning.

Papa Darling stepped out of his study. "Are we in a total preparedness situation, my dear?" he said.

"My dress!" cried Mrs. Darling. "My jewels! My hair!"

"My impression is that your appearance is highly acceptable," said Papa Darling, brushing feebly at a splash of custard. He looked at his watch and frowned. "We are in a negative punctuality situation."

"Brute!" cried Mrs. Darling.

Papa Darling helped her up. He knew he had said the wrong thing, and he was going to take it out on someone. He turned his eye on Nanny Dodgson, moaning, electrocuted, custard soaked, concussed. "You," he said. "You are to be outwardly redeployed as part of an ad hoc child-care-staff downsizing."

"Pardon?" bubbled Nanny Dodgson.

"You're fired."

"Nooo!" cried Mrs. Darling. "You don't know what you're doing! You didn't hear what the agency said last time. She's our last hope. They'll never—"

"Hush, little one," said Papa Darling, using the exact masterful tone he had used to summon Mrs. Darling from the typing pool that marvelous morning they had first met. "Outsourcing is a major part of my skill profile, as you are aware. Using these skills, I shall find another child-care operative. Out of my house, wicked Nanny Dodgson! Now, this instant!"

Daisy was watching from high up at the nursery window as Nanny Dodgson reeled out of the front door. "Steady," she said. "Steady. Bombs away." Cassian released the extra-heavy loaf of bread Primrose had baked specially. They watched it fall, fifteen meters straight down, onto the center of the custard-splattered bowler hat. They watched the nanny knees buckle. They watched the nanny uniform sprawl in the gutter. They turned away from the window, dusting their hands.

Five minutes later, ambulance sirens filled the street. The children picked up their books of hard sums and waited, good as gold, for the feet on the stairs.

"When will they ever *learn?*" sighed Daisy.

"Come on," said Papa Darling. "We're going to be late."

"But you don't understand!" moaned Mrs. Darling. "Those nanny agencies won't—they warned me last time. . . ."

"Incorrect, my dove," said Papa Darling, who believed everything could be fixed as long as he was the one trying to fix it, using money. "You go and redeploy your personal grooming. I shall initiate a resolution to our personnel problem."

"But—"

"Shoo, little woman!" cried Papa Darling. And Mrs. Darling shooed, shaking her head and muttering darkly. She did not like being called little woman or told to shoo. When she had been Papa Darling's secretary, she had run his life. Who did he think he was? Well, let him find out for himself, and then she could have a little bit of a gloat. They would be late for Lady Mortdarthur's party, but that would allow her to make a grand entrance. It was the perfect night to wear her sapphires.

Papa Darling dialed.

"Nenny Acedemy," said a woman's voice, very prim.

"Good evening," said Papa Darling. "I am seeking to appoint a child-care-assistance operative, experience crucial, ability to grow in post essential, no time wasters." A picture of his children rose in his mind, dimly, because he had not met them recently. "Anyone you've got. Ten minutes would be about right. Number One, Avenue Marshal Posh: it's the biggest house in the town, gold Roller in the driveway, you can't miss it."

"So," said the voice, which now sounded like a prim glacier. "Am I speaking to Mr. Darling?"

"You are engaged in an ongoing dialogue with that self-same person. But you can call me Colin."

"Ai have no desire to call you anything whatever, Mr. Darling. Ai have to inform you that Nanny Dodgson has just been brought back here in a state of collapse and when she leaves hospital will need complete reprogramming. Like, I may say, her seventeen predecessors in your employ."

"Listen," said Papa Darling. "The remuneration package will be highly attractive. We are talking double wages; tell a lie, triple. Plus bonus, free access to wine cellar and choc locker, latest model Honda Aerodeck—"

But the Nanny Academy had hung up.

"Tch!" said Papa Darling. "Poor communication skills. Well, plenty of fish in the sea." Peering at the yellow pages, he dialed the next number.

And the next.

And the one after that, and the one after that.

Acme Nursery Staff said that unfortunately all their nannies had suddenly gone down with a mystery virus. Babychums Unlimited, on hearing his name, started suddenly to pretend they were an answering machine. Child-Care Specialists hung up on him. And Never Mind Nannies seemed to have got the same virus as Acme Nursery Staff.

Papa Darling pulled at his lower lip. His years of management experience had not prepared him for this. He dialed Expert Nursery Logistics. ENL gave him the chill, too. He said to the usual prim voice on the far end, "I am having some difficulty in interpreting this negative response situation."

"I beg your pardon?"

"Why can't I get a bleeding nanny for my nippers, 'scuse my French?"

There was a sharp nanny sniff. "I could not say," answered the voice.

"All right," said Papa Darling. "Are we on some sort of blacklist?"

Silence. Then the voice, slimy as a society eel. "Put it like this, Mr., er, Darling. You are indeed on a Nanny Network list and, as you have correctly surmised, it is by no means a white list. Good evening to you." *Click* went the telephone, and *hum* went the dial tone.

"Coo-ee," said the suspiciously sweet voice of Papa's little woman on the stairs. "Solved my little problem, have you? Are you read-ee, Papa?"

Daisy was scowling at the fire. Cassian was in the corner, welding teeth onto a mousetrap. Primrose was at her Doll's Kitchen Wee Stove, shaking dark brown powder into a cake mixture from a jar labeled OPIUM.

"I wonder what the next one'll be like," said Daisy gloomily.

"Whoever she is, we'll be ready for her," said Primrose, stirring with both her little white hands.

"Amazing they can find 'em, really," said Cassian, pushing up his welder's mask. "I mean, I wouldn't look after us, would you?"

"Certainly not," said Daisy, horrified. "They'll get someone, though. They'll have to. Can you imagine them not going out every night? Can you imagine actually *talking* to them?"

There was a silence.

Nobody could.

Papa Darling had not got hugely, insanely, bloatedly rich by giving up easily. His new wife's voice, sweet, cracked, and tough as overcooked toffee, reminded him that in the matter of finding a replacement nanny, he faced humiliation. Panic fluttered in his breast. *Me?* he thought, chief executive officer of Darling Gigantic, a major player in the expanding nature-reserve concreting field, get done over by an old crow in brogues and wool stockings? No way, José. Do me a favor.

But what was he going to do? He could ring up Miss Excellent, his devoted, hideous, handpicked new secretary, and insist that she come in and babysit. Then he had a vision of Miss Excellent's patient face horizontal, the rest of her trussed to the rotisserie in the stainless steel kitchen, with Cassian bypassing the safety switches, Daisy sharpening a carving knife, and Primrose making pencil notes in a book on sauces for meat. Little scallywags, he thought, almost (but not quite) fondly. Plus, good secretaries were hard to find and harder to keep.

At this point his eye fell on an advertisement so huge that he had not even noticed it before. It covered an entire yellow page at the beginning of the Child-Care section. *AAA Aardvark Child Minding and Security,* it read. *We Understand the Problems of the Wealthy. Keen Rates. Unaffiliated. Forget the Rest, Hire the Best. Royal Refrinces Available . . .*

But Papa Darling had stopped reading at the word *unaffiliated.* Unaffiliated meant, if he had read it right, that AAA Aardvark was not connected to the Nanny Network. No Nanny Network, no blacklist.

He was already dialing.

The telephone on the other end rang for a long time. Finally, a man's voice said, "Yeah?"

"Is this AAA Aardvark?"

"What if it is?" said the voice, and sniffed, long and bubbly.

This was not a tone that Papa Darling expected from nanny agencies, no matter how unaffiliated. But they were already two minutes late for dinner. So he said, "I have a nanny requirement."

"Pardon?"

"I . . . we . . . need a nanny."

"When?"

"In the short to medium term."

"Come again?"

"Ten minutes, max."

The voice sucked its teeth. "Dunno," it said. "I mean, we've got Nanny Big Georgina out at the Queen of Tonga's, lovely little saucepans—"

"What?"

"Saucepan lids. Kids. Plus we've got Nanny Doberman out at Hoxton with Mad Dave the Artist, nasty little ankle biters, but we have hopes the rabies injections may take this time. Maybe we could fit you in Tuesday."

"An interesting point of view," said Papa Darling. "And if we modify it a little, I feel sure that we can arrive at a meaningful consensus—"

"Huh?" said the voice.

"Listen, sunshine," said Papa Darling, low and danger-ous. "Me and my lady wife are going out to dinner with the kind of people you can only dream about meeting, and we want one of your little people round here yesterday or some-what sooner. Are you with me?"

Something happened to the voice. "Ooh," it said, with a note like the coo of a London pigeon. "Out to dinner, sir, or should I say, my lord? You should have said earlier. AAA Aardvark will of course have great pleasure in putting on our, ahem, emergency special service in the person of Nanny Pete, which is to say Miss Petronella Fryer. And what address would that be at, Your Highness?"

Papa Darling found himself suddenly liking this unconven-tional but respectful person. "Number One, Avenue Marshal Posh," he said.

There was a pause, into which Papa Darling read admira-tion. The voice turned to even more syrup. "Is that right?" it said. "Very nice, if I may make so bold as to remark. Nanny Fryer will be round as soon as she has popped her stun gun in her ditty bag, to coin a phrase, heh, heh."

"Make it so," said smug Papa Darling, and put down the phone. Funny, they normally asked for money.

"Well?" said Mrs. Secretary Darling, not toffee anymore, but broken glass. "You haven't found anybody, and bang goes dinner. I told you, nannies, they're like gold dust. Men. You just don't underst—"

"Darling," said Papa Darling. He was going to make a remark about his life being enhanced by her luxurious personal adornment strategy, but she was glittering so powerfully he thought he might have some kind of epileptic fit. This was one of those times when only plain language would do. "Blow me down," he said, shading his eyes with his hand. "You are looking proper radiant, my love. I always did say that sapphires go lovely with diamonds, and the cabochon rubies are just the finishing touch. Nanny Fryer will be round in five."

The children sat on the nursery windowsill, banging their heels against the brickwork and scowling into the dark void of Avenue Marshal Posh—strictly against the rules, of course, but there was no nanny to tell them what the rules actually were. A black sedan came round the corner on two wheels and stopped at the curb with a screech of brakes.

"Funny car," said Daisy.

"Jaguar," said Cassian. "Mark 2, split windscreen. Classic bank robbers' getaway vehicle. Needs new piston rings."

The doors of the Jaguar burst open. A figure stumbled out into the road and stood hunched against the breeze. It was wearing a brown bowler hat. From up here, everyone looked stocky. Not as stocky as that, though.

"Looks nervous," said Cassian, focusing his night glasses.

"Should hope so, too," said Primrose.

The nanny pulled something out of her bag, something

that glinted in the light that shone from the Darlings' huge French windows. She raised it to her mouth and jerked her head back. "Whiskey," said Cassian. "Old Sporran."

"Poor benighted woman," sighed Daisy. "Here she comes."

The nanny had wiped her mouth with the back of her hand, squared her broad shoulders, and marched up the marble front steps. Far below in the house, the doorbell rang.

"They're off!" cried Primrose.

Sure enough, the front door was opening, and Mrs. Secretary Darling, a vision in gold Lurex, was gliding toward the Rolls. Behind her came Papa Darling, looking, as usual, at his watch.

"Nana!" they cried sweetly, scooping up a cushion each and hauling open the nursery door.

The Darling children had a well-established routine for greeting new nannies.

What happened was this.

The banisters of the splendid oval staircase made a gleaming helix of mahogany all the way from the nursery floor to the hall. "Saddle up!" cried Daisy, who had seen *The Charge of the Light Brigade*, a film approved of by nannies.

The children slapped their cushions on the polished mahogany.

"By numbers, mount, walk, trot. One!"

Cassian was One. He broke into a run, pushing his

cushion along the rail. When he reached the top stair, he leaped onto it so he was sitting astride the banister, facing downward, accelerating down the wooden slope, while behind him Daisy yelled, "Two!" and Primrose climbed aboard, "Three!" and then climbed on herself. Then they were all hurtling downward, faster and faster, yelling, "*Chaaarge!*"

Cassian had calculated terminal velocity at 31.03 miles per hour. Whatever it was, nannies found it most upsetting. Nanny Danvers had scuttled hastily out of the door without even putting down her suitcase. Nanny Dredd had pretended not to have noticed anything was amiss, got Cassian's boots slap in the centerline, and been removed to the Nanny Sanatorium in two separate ambulances. Normally, nannies with good reflexes dived under the heavy marble-and-gilt hall table. They never really recovered their dignity.

This one was different.

With the usual great cry of, "*Banzai!*" a solid battering ram of children whizzed off the bottom of the banisters and shot feet first toward where the new nanny should have been standing in her brogues, saying, "Prune," and smiling at the same time, as only nannies can.

But there was no nanny. Instead, Cassian noticed an abnormal pile of cushions that someone had put to break his impact. Then he and his sisters landed with a *whump.*

As Cassian sorted out his legs from those of the girls, he could hear them talking. "Interesting," Daisy was saying, in the tone of voice that meant she was working out what made someone tick. "Very interesting."

Primrose was readjusting her Alice band and smiling sweetly. "From now on," she muttered, "no more Mr. Nice Guy."

But Cassian was watching the nanny.

She was short and wider than any nanny he had ever seen. She was standing just inside the door of the dining room. One of the sideboard drawers was open. The nanny had a jeweler's glass screwed into her eye and was squinting at a handful of cutlery. Feeling Cassian watching her, she looked up. "Hello," she said. "And who are you?"

"Mind your own business," said Cassian, anxious to get on the right footing after the failure of the Charge.

"What do you think you're doing?" said Primrose.

"Jus' looking around," said the nanny. "Scouting out the lie of the land, like. Very nice class of spoon here, if I may make so bold as to pass comment."

"You may not," said Daisy. The children gave her the Silent Stare. The nanny eased her tight starched collar and looked slightly flustered. Daisy said, "What are you called?"

"Nanny First Class Petronella Fryer," said the nanny. "But you can call me Pete."

"It is time for our nice supper, Nanny Fryer," said Daisy, still freezing.

"Oh, ah," said Nanny Fryer. "What d'you fancy, then?"

There was a stunned silence. Nannies did not ask you; they told you. Daisy dug the others with her elbows. It was probably a trick. They would ask for chicken, chips, strawberries, and cream, and the nanny would give them lumpy porridge and burnt custard anyway.

"We don't know," said Daisy, simpering horribly. "We're shy, you see."

Nanny Fryer had been gaping round the hall at the statues and chandeliers, whistling a little tune. Now she took her chin between her thumb and forefinger. There was a distinct rasp of stubble, which was odd, because most nannies didn't shave, not even ones like Nanny Clamp, who needed to. "Tellyawhat," said the nanny, pulling out a mobile phone. "We can do Indian, Chinese, or pizza."

More silence, genuinely baffled this time. Finally, Daisy said, "We've never had Indian."

"Nor Chinese either," said Cassian.

"What's pizza?" said Primrose.

The nanny drew down eyebrows huge even by nanny standards. She went to the drinks tray and poured herself a stiff whiskey. She picked up the telephone, dialed Khan's, Lee Ho Fook's, and Antonio's, and talked to each of them for five minutes. When she had finished, she turned with a kindly twinkle in her eye and said, "Kids, tonight is the first night of the rest of your lives. The future starts here."

The children sat stunned. They had been ready to massacre this nanny as usual. But somehow they could not think of anything to say.

Except something they had never, ever said in all their lives.

"Yes, Nanny," they said.

It was some evening.

The food took a bit of getting used to for children whose normal diet was Irish stew and burnt rice pudding. But it was good stuff, packed with many flavors, particularly the pineapple, peppermint, and tuna fish pizza. And it was even better when you ate it in the big drawing room, sitting on bearskins (Papa Darling shot a lot of bears, mostly from helicopters) round the fire, spitting chicken bones and olive pips into the flames of the Kosiglo Massive Inferno gas-log hearth.

Daisy asked Nanny Pete a lot of questions. Unlike most nannies, who were of the opinion that curiosity killed the cat, Nanny Pete actually answered. Though on the whole the answers were quite hard to understand. From what she said, it sounded as if Nanny Pete had looked after a lot of horses and playing cards as well as children. Daisy could not quite work out how it all fitted together. Besides which, Cassian kept interrupting to find out how the card games worked, and Primrose kept on butting in to ask whether everybody thought the red stuff on the tandoori chicken was ketchup or varnish or a mixture of the two. Still, they got on famously. And Daisy had the distinct impression that Nanny Pete was just as curious about the little Darlings as the little Darlings were about Nanny Pete. Which for a nanny was odd, going on totally weird.

Still, there was not much time to think about weirdness. First, Nanny Pete gave a small but seamanlike exhibition of hornpipe dancing. Then she outlined the rules of poker—the children caught on fast, and Nanny declared the game closed after she had lost £11.50 and said she saw great futures ahead for them. Then they all did more hornpipe dancing. All in all, the big drawing room, with its black marble floor and hugely expensive paintings of fat ladies with no clothes on, had never witnessed such a scene. When the dancing was finished, everyone chatted and laughed. Nanny Pete leaned back in a gold brocade armchair with a silver tankard of Papa Darling's Rare Old Port and lit a Capstan Full Strength. She pointed to the piano. "Gissa tune, someone."

"Can't," said Daisy. "And anyway, it's out of tune."

"Out of tune?"

"Ever since Mummy left. Real Mummy. Ages ago. We don't remember. She used to play it. 'Stand by Me' was her favorite tune, Papa said once. They used to sing it together. Then Mummy went away and Papa started up with Secretary Mummy and now Papa won't let anyone touch the piano."

"Shame, choice joanna like that," said Nanny Pete. "Well, kids, what time do you like to garden up the apples?"

"Uh?"

"Garden hoe. Go. Apples and pears. Stairs. The wooden hill to Bedfordshire. To bye-byes."

"Oh, sometime about midnight," said Cassian.

"If not later," said Daisy hastily.

"When we feel like it, really," said Primrose. This nanny seemed to be a lot better than the others, but there was no sense letting your guard down. The Darlings had had nannies for long enough to have learned that kindliness was the same as weakness.

Nanny Pete drained her port, belched, and pitched her cigarette butt into the Kosiglo. "Tough," she said. "New regime. It's off you go. Now."

"Oh, Nana," whined the children like one child. Daisy caught Cassian's eye. Cassian nudged Primrose. They all went and clung to Nanny Pete, saying, "Nana," and, "Pleeease," and, "You promised." Nanny Pete actually blushed, as if she were not used to this sort of treatment. Daisy went "Gidgygidgygidgy," and tickled her ribs.

"Hee, hee, hee," went Nanny Pete, poor unsuspecting creature.

For Daisy had given the signal. And while Primrose and Cassian tickled Nanny, Daisy's skilled hands went through the pockets of her uniform. It was a routine they always used with a nanny who showed any sign of weakness.

Nanny Pete heaved herself up, shedding little Darlings like a mountain shedding stones. "Oi!" she cried. "Off!"

And off they scampered up the stairs, shrieking with childish glee.

"Nanny will be up in ten!" cried the voice from below.

The nursery door closed. "Right," said Cassian, wiping the gooby look from his face. "Leave it to me. Ready in five."

"Check," said Primrose.

"Check what?" said Daisy. "Oh, no. Not the Junior Car Thief Kit again."

But Cassian was already busy. He opened an Action Man box in the corner of the nursery. Inside the box was not a plastic idiot in camo trousers, but a key copier Cassian had assembled from an Erector set and parts of a kitchen blender Cook thought she had thrown away. Into the machine he clamped the key Daisy had stolen from Nanny's pockets— the key, if he was not mistaken, to the truly excellent Jaguar in which Nanny Pete had arrived.

Most nanny cars he had stolen had been small and feeble, appallingly tidy, and painted beige. Cassian really fancied a go in a Jag.

He made two copies of the key. As he was putting the machine away, heavy brogues crunched on the stairs. "Coming!" hissed Daisy. She and Primrose were already in their beds in the night nursery. Cassian leaped into his pajamas without touching the sides and hurled himself into bed.

"All right!" cried Nanny Pete. "Into your pits, the lot of you!"

"We already are, Nana dear," said Daisy. "Aren't we, children? And we've brushed our teeth."

"And our hair, a hundred times," said Primrose.

"And our shoes," said Cassian sickeningly. The children lay there good as gold, with the sheets pulled up tight under their little chins.

"Kiss us good night, Nana!" said Daisy.

Nanny Pete said something under her breath. It sounded like, "Ugh." She took a deep breath and kissed Daisy. Then she kissed Primrose. Then she went to kiss Cassian. But Cassian said, "Yuck," and pushed her away. As he did so, he secretly dropped the car key back in her pocket.

"Shy boy!" said Nanny Pete, sounding strangely relieved.

"Tell us a story, Nanny Pete!" cried Primrose.

"Don't know any," said Nanny Pete.

"Sing a song, then!"

"Ah," said Nanny Pete. "Yur. Mi-mi-mi-mi-mi-mi-mi-miiii. Ahem." In a strangely gruff voice, she began to sing:

Restez endormis, mes enfants,
défense de s'égarer la nuit,

car des millions de voleurs immondes
se trouvent blottis au fond de vos lits [*]

It went on like this for some time.

"What does that mean?" said Primrose.

"It's French," said Nanny Pete. "Read the footnote later."

"It was lovely," said Daisy, who was not used to bedtime songs.

But Nanny Pete was gone.

They heard her stump into the day nursery. They heard the slight clatter as she put up the gold-plated fireguard. They heard running water and clanking as she washed up the pigeon fork in the nursery sink. Then there was more shuffling, a sharp exclamation, and the scrape of a chair.

"What's she doing?" said Primrose.

"Straightening pictures," said Daisy.

Nannies loved things to be in straight lines. Things were normal again. The children lay there for a moment, happy and reassured, until the nanny brogues had receded downstairs.

Then Cassian was up, followed by Primrose, then Daisy.

The pictures in the nursery were very straight, the fireguard gleaming, all traces of pigeon grease gone from the grate. Cassian and Primrose naturally did not waste time admiring all this spick-and-span-ness. They beetled toward the door,

---

[*] *Go to sleep, my children*
  No wandering in the night
  Because of the millions of filthy thieves
  To be found crouched at the foot of your beds

jaws set, narrow-eyed and determined, like you had to be when you were off to twock a Jag.

"Wait," said Daisy.

Her brother and sister turned. She was frowning at the wall, one beautifully manicured fingernail on her pretty chin. "Something's wrong," she said.

Primrose said, "It always looks bad when they do that to the pictures."

"No," said Daisy. "It's the Bear's Bum."

"Uh?"

"It's gone." She waved an elegant hand at a bare space on the wall. "Used to be there," she said. "Is there no longer."

"Probably cleaning it," said Primrose. "Dusty ol' thing."

"They're always cleaning things," said Cassian.

Still, Daisy thought it was odd. Nobody knew what the Bear's Bum was for, really. It had a reputation for being expensive, goodness knew why. There were a lot of things on the walls at Number One, Avenue Marshal Posh, simply because they were expensive. After a while, you gave up asking, because some nanny would tell you curiosity killed the cat, and even if you got an answer, you could be pretty certain it would be too boring to understand. There was something else about the Bear's Bum, though. It had arrived very soon after Real Mummy had disappeared. . . .

Did I not tell you? Sorry.

The first Mrs. Darling had been a kind person—everything a mother should have been, in fact, except that the nannies locked her out of the nursery. One day, without saying anything to anyone, she had gone. Soon after she had gone, the Bear's Bum had arrived.

And from about the time of the arrival of the Bear's Bum (it was hard to remember, exactly; they had been so young), the little Darlings had been brought up by nannies. Their upper lips were stiff, their shoes brushed and shining. If they Made a Fuss, they Went to Bed Without Their Suppers.

So they became nicely brought up children. They were Seen and not Heard, they Minded their Manners, and they were Upstairs in the Nursery. Silent, polite, and invisible, they took a terrible revenge on all nannies.

Now, they crept silently downstairs. Clanking noises came from the dining room as they crept across the hall. Noiselessly, they opened the front door. Keeping in the shadow of some enormously expensive bushes, they crept up to the car.

It was a beautiful thing, gleaming black in the streetlamps, giving off a faint, sharp reek of burnt castor oil. "Race tuned!" said Cassian.

"As if you knew what that meant," said Daisy.

"It's just a car," said Primrose. "And it smells."

"You wait," said Cassian, and he put one of the duplicate keys in the door. The locks opened with a deep, heavy clunk. "Custom," said Cassian. "Hop in, girls."

This was the bit the girls hated, because Cassian might be

a brilliant mechanic, but he was an awful driver, and besides, he was not really tall enough to reach the pedals.

"I'm feeling sick," said Primrose.

"Sicken chicken," said Cassian, shutting the doors so they were three abreast across the front and leaning forward to put the key in the ignition.

"Well, I'm going back to bed," said Daisy, "and poo to your silly old Jag—oh, hell."

The front door had opened. Nanny Pete was standing on the doorstep. She looked a little unsteady. Perhaps it was the whiskey and port. Or perhaps it was because of the enormous sack she carried over her shoulder.

"Wha . . . ?" said Cassian.

"Down," said Daisy, quicker thinking. And all three of them leaped into the back and squeezed down behind the front seats.

"Hold your breath," hissed Daisy.

Keys rattled outside. A voice, muffled by steel and glass, hummed a tune.

The boot opened.

There followed a great clanking and grunting, as if someone were trying to jam a very big thing into a very small space. Cassian knew what was happening. "'The Jaguar Mark 2, while in almost every respect the ideal vehicle, suffers from a boot space more suited to the casual weekender than the serious touring motorist,'" he whispered, quoting from one of the huge pile of car magazines in his room. "'The backseat space, however—'"

Someone swore. The back door opened. Something that felt like a metal landslide buried the children. Daisy felt an elbow in her ribs.

"What?" she hissed.

"There's somefing in my mouf," said Primrose. "Ptoo. It's all fmelly and horrid and dufty. I fink—"

She stopped, because the driver's door had opened. Someone heavy plumped onto the driver's seat. The starter coughed. The engine roared. Tires squealed as the Jag shot away from the curb in a perfect getaway, Nanny Pete's brown bowler hat low over the steering wheel.

"What's happening?" said Cassian, under the thunder of the V6 engine.

"It's like this," whispered Daisy, who had been working things out. "That nanny isn't a nanny. She pretended to be a nanny to get into the house and she's pinched everything and she thinks we're all safely tucked up in bed. But instead, thanks to your stupid car thing, Cassian, we are on our way to a whatever-you-call-it of burglars."

There was a long, thoughtful silence, except for the mighty roar of the engine. Primrose finally managed to get whatever it was out of her mouth. Her fingers felt plush and a mahogany shield with a label on it. It was the Bear's Bum. "A den of burglars," she said.

"Stolen goods," said Cassian.

"Secretary Mummy and Papa will be horrified," said Daisy.

Another pause. Then, all together in the silence under the huge sack of silver, they whispered, "Fantastic!"

But Cassian's mind was only partly on what he was saying.

As they had shot out of the drive, he had managed to peer out of the window and had seen something most peculiar.

A large, pale vehicle had drawn up under the trees up the road. It had looked like an enormous van. A white van, with rusty wheel arches. As the Jag had shot down the road, the sides of the van had dropped, turning into ramps. Down the ramps had rolled big machines. They had looked like a digger, a dumper, and a dozer, and they had turned in between the twin gate lodges of Number One, Avenue Marshal Posh. Nanny Pete had glanced round. Cassian had seen her bare her teeth and say, "Heh, heh!"

Then the Jag had turned a corner, and it had all been hidden.

It was odd. Very odd.

Lady Mortdarthur's had been a bit of all right, definitely. Mr. Darling had worked out that he was richer than anyone else in that roomful of very rich people. This was always nice. And Lady Alfonsine de Luxe, on seeing Mrs. Darling's subtle blend of gold Lurex, diamonds, rubies, and sapphires, had put on dark glasses. That was always nice, too.

"Ooh, Papa, if only tonight would never stop!" cried Mrs. Darling in the car afterward.

"It can be conveniently transformed into an ongoing situation," said Mr. Darling, whipping out his mobile. When he had finished talking, he blew into the speaking tube and roared, "Chauffeur!"

"Aye, aye, sir," said the chauffeur, dabbing his spitty ear with a handkerchief.

"Airport!" barked Mr. Darling. "First-class Caribbean departures!"

"Caribbean?" said Mrs. Darling.

"Antigua for breakfast," said Mr. Darling. "Sun, sand, a beach-concreting initiative. We deserve it."

"Ooh, yes. And I can buy whatever I need. . . ." Mrs. Darling sank into a pink dream of shopping. Then she said, "But what about the children?"

"The nanny will take care of them. Nice woman." Mr. Darling preened himself. "I am, as you know, not inexperienced in the human resources sphere. Highly skilled judge of character."

"Yes, dear," said Mrs. Darling. But she still sounded unsure.

"And I tell you what," said Mr. Darling. "When we get to Antigua, we'll send them a picture postcard."

Mrs. Darling beamed. Never let it be said she did not care for her husband's kids, whatever their names were. "Ooh, you are clever," she said, snuggling up against him. "Papa Darling, you are the bestest papa in the whole wide world!"

It is not at all easy to see where you are going when you are facedown under a wheelbarrow load of precious metals and a Bear's Bum on the rear footwell of a Mark 2 Jaguar. On the whole, the best you can do is listen.

The sounds were confusing. There was the engine, of course, a great throaty roar. Then there was something that sounded like a town, with honking horns and a railway bridge, and a lot of stopping and starting, probably at traffic lights. After that there were a lot of corners and voices shouting in foreign languages. Finally there was a bump and a rumble, as if the wheels were traveling over cobbles, and the Jaguar came to a halt.

The driver's door opened and shut. Nanny Pete's footsteps crunched away into the distance. Cassian found that by wriggling his shoulders, he could make a little space under the avalanche of silver and gold. He forced his head between the door and the Homebuilders' Federation Challenge Cup awarded to Papa Darling for the massacre of three endangered species. Finally, he could see out.

"Golly," he said, and fell into an astonished silence.

"What is it?" said Daisy, pinching his leg.

But her brother was too astounded to speak.

The Jaguar was parked on a cobbled quay. A full moon shone from a cloudless sky. It glittered on the waters of a broad, inky creek, lined with buildings deadly gray under the cold kiss of its light. Nothing moved on the surface of the creek except the wavelets, always shifting, always the same.

Nanny Pete was walking down a set of rusty railway lines toward a high wall. The wall was part of an enormous building covered with turrets and little spires. It might have been the chancy shadows of the moonlight. But it seemed to Cassian that there had once been writing up there, enormous writing, on the broad band of masonry that divided a row of smashed and sagging oriel windows (like blisters, he thought) from a rank of buttresses (like the roots of some awful spooky stone tree, he thought).

Nanny Pete arrived at a gigantic double door studded with nails.

"What is it?" hissed Daisy, pinching Cassian again.

Cassian described the scene.

Daisy said, "I'm not sure about this."

"I am," said Primrose.

"That is because you are too young to know any better."

"Oooooh!" said Primrose and Cassian, both together. "Listen to Nana!"

Daisy felt a hot blush of shame mount her cheeks. They were right, of course. As the eldest, one sometimes forgot oneself and had what almost amounted to nanny thoughts. "I do beg your pardon," she said.

"Think nothing of it," said Cassian.

"One understands perfectly," said Primrose.

"The point is this," said Cassian. "There is nowhere to hide. If we run away now, she will drive after us and catch us."

Daisy made the tutting sound that elder sisters have made ever since their younger brothers suggested that saber-toothed tiger skins would make really nice rugs for the cave floor. "And if we don't and she takes us through that door?"

"We'll be in the den," said Cassian.

"Loot," said Primrose. "Piles of it."

"And the Bear's Bum is here."

"That is indeed slightly mysterious."

"I suppose it is."

There was a silence as their thoughts gently circled the bum, and its appearance back in the fog of extreme youth, and its attempted theft tonight.

"Hmm," said Daisy after a longish pause. "So we follow the bum?"

"Might as well," said Primrose.

"Shhh!" said Cassian.

Nanny Pete had turned a vast key in one of the doors. She was trundling it open. The arch opened, a gaping mouth of darkness. She started back to the car.

Cassian gasped and turned a silver ice bucket over his head so he would not have to look. In the moonlight, he had seen a terrible thing.

Nanny Pete had taken off her bowler hat.

Nannies always had nice brown hair, which they brushed tidily and did up in nets so it looked like horse dung.

But Nanny Pete's head shone pale as an egg under the moon.

Nanny Pete was bald.

The driver's door slammed. The engine roared. Nanny

Pete drove through the doors, pulled them to, and locked them. The Jag moved forward. The horn blatted, dit, dit, dit, dah. There was a winding, grinding noise that filled the car.

"This is getting a bit terrifying," said Daisy, muffled under the silverware.

"More than a bit," hissed Primrose.

"Just about completely," whispered Cassian.

"Interesting, though," murmured Daisy.

"Makes a change," hissed Primrose.

"You bet your sweet bottom," whispered Cassian.

"Cassian!" hissed his sisters.

"Beg your pardon," whispered Cassian. "Over-excited."

"Us too," hissed Primrose and Daisy.

There was a great and very interesting sound of grinding machinery. "What now?" said Cassian aloud.

Daisy came to a decision. "Heave!" she said. The three children heaved and surfaced in a glittering swamp of precious metal.

"Oi!" said Nanny Pete, turning round so fast they heard her neck click. There was something tattooed on the crown of her skull. An eagle, now Daisy came to look at it.

"You're a man!" cried Primrose.

"Course I am," said Nanny Pete, who had a dazed look. "And who are you?"

"The Darling children, Nana," they said all together.

"Stone me," said Nanny Pete. "So you are."

They began to babble sweetly; obviously, childishness was the only solution here. "Don't you remember? You came to our house and dodged the Charge and bought us weird food and put us to bed and sang us a song. . . ."

"And swiped the spoons," said Cassian coolly.

"And the Bear's Bum," said Daisy.

Until that moment, Nanny Pete had been leaning back in the driver's seat, cleaning his fingernails with a flick knife. Now he clicked the knife shut with a horribly practiced jerk of the wrist and slid it smoothly up the starched cuff of his nanny blouse. "What about the Bear's Bum?" he said.

This might be a man with an eagle tattooed on his shaved head. But it was also a person dressed in a nanny uniform and therefore a Legitimate Target. "Bear's bum?" they said, using the old "Mention It, Get It Mentioned Back, and Deny All Knowledge" technique, which had put Nanny De'Ath into a lunatic asylum after two weeks.

Nanny Pete shook his head, as if puzzled. "I did ought to take you straight home," he said. "Only it's not as easy as that."

"Anyway," said Daisy, "you've brought us, and now we'd like to stay a little."

"I should say so," said Nanny Pete grimly. "I mean, that would be very nice."

"Oh, thank you, Nana!" chorused the Darling children excitedly.

"Less of the Nana," said Pete.

The children nodded. Each knew that this should all be rather worrying, but each was busy with private thoughts. Primrose was wondering if getting a tattoo on your head hurt a lot, because sometimes she felt she had had enough of Alice bands and mild pink complexions. Cassian was admiring the gigantic crane that was lowering a cargo net from far overhead and wondering what sort of building it was that they were parked next to. As usual, Daisy was thinking about the situation and devising ways to get answers to some of the thousands of questions in her mind. "You're probably wondering what to do with us," she said.

"Too right," said Nanny Pete.

"You'll have to be nice to us, of course," said Daisy.

"You're not in your mansion now," said Pete. "I could knock you on the head and roll you into the 'oggin, no worries."

"'Oggin?" said Daisy.

"'Oggin," said Nanny Pete, "is what us seagoing folk call the sea."

"Oh no, you could not," said Daisy, though actually she was not feeling 100 percent confident. They were in a strange car, behind studded doors, and the cargo net was very close.

Tch, she told herself. Look on the bright side. They were on their own. There was no nanny, unless you counted Pete, which she did not, and no parents. It was a state of affairs they had been longing for for years.

"So what," said Pete, "is stopping me drowning you, then?"

"Oh, really," said Daisy, with an impatient click of the tongue. "You're a burglar, not a murderer. What about your professional pride?"

"Good point," said Pete. "But maybe I'm a murderer, too. Multitasking, like."

"Never," said Daisy, though her mouth was frankly rather dry.

"'Scuse me a minute," said Pete. The cargo net was down now. The children saw there were two men hanging onto its sides. One of them was only a meter high. Both had shaved heads and tattoos. They began to secure the net around the car. "Make her fast and up she goes."

"Hoftages?" said the meter-high man, who had no teeth, as he peered through the window of the Jag.

"Hostages," replied Pete, chuckling horribly. Daisy thought the horribleness sounded forced.

"He's fibbing," said Daisy. "We're guests. Honored ones. Take her up, boys."

"Oi!" said Pete, and Daisy had a very strong feeling that she was right and that beneath that tattooed exterior lurked a geezer of purest diamond.

The net was secure round the Jag, and the ground was already sinking away from them.

"Listen," hissed Pete. "This wasn't my idea. All I want is a nice quiet life. I'll take you home, right?"

"We don't want to go home," said Primrose. "If you take us back, we'll turn you in. Stitch you up like a kipper."

There was a silence, except for the grinding of the crane. Daisy tried to concentrate on what would happen at the top. There were, however, distractions.

The wall up which they were being lifted was perhaps thirty meters high. Now that they were up here, they could see that they were passing rows of round brass portholes. There were lights on in some of them. Through one, Primrose saw an enormous cast-iron kitchen stretching away to vanishing point. Through another, Cassian saw polished brass generators. "Ooh!" cried Daisy as they passed a ballroom.

"It's a ship," said Cassian.

It certainly was a ship, an absolutely enormous ship. They rose past decks, galleries, lifeboats. They caught a glimpse of great round funnels towering among wreaths of steam. Far below, shrunk to a ribbon with distance, was the quay. Glancing across at Pete, Daisy saw that a sort of soupy grin had pasted itself to his face. The burglar was proud of the ship, it seemed. Daisy decided to win him over. "This is the most amazing thing I have ever seen," she said.

"It is, innit?" said Pete, blushing slightly. "SS *Kleptomanic*. We are alongside in the private docks of the Transglobal Steamship Company, once the pride of the fleet, now the property of AAA Aardvark Child Minding and Security."

"So how did you get hold of the ship?"

"We nicked it. Sort of."

"What do you mean, sort of?"

Pete blushed. "Just nicked it."

"But it's still here."

"Yeah," said Pete. "Story of our life."

"Brilliant," said Daisy, rather sarcastically.

"No need to be like that," said Pete, wounded. "We're getting better all the time. I'll explain when we get there."

A face appeared at the window. "He'f right, you know," said the very small person with no teeth clinging to the cargo net. "Practiff makef perfect. Fcufe me. Couldn't help overhearing. Nosy Clanger, at your ferviff. Coming in to land any minute."

And indeed the net with the Jag was now swinging over shuffleboard courts and a swimming pool full of what looked like coal, toward a green deck with a white *J* painted on it.

And landing.

Five men with wheelbarrows appeared. They emptied the backseat of the car of silver and gold and carried the Bear's Bum away with strange reverence. There was only enough gold and silver to fill three and a half barrows. "Is that all?" said Nosy. He sounded disappointed.

"Certainly is," said Nanny Pete defensively.

"Oh. Great. Only . . ."

"Yeah?"

"Well, it'f not much, if it? I mean there muft of been Turkish carpetf, a ftereo, couple of tellief, free peef fweet and vat. And what about the fafe?"

Pete was scowling horribly. "Listen," he said. "I am there in a brown bowler hat in a strange house. I do my best. I got the Bear's Bum."

"You got vat?" said Nosy. "Unbleeble. Waf it—?"

"Shhh," said Pete, jerking his head at his passengers. "So anyway, when I get in, I reckon I've got approx three hours to get it done because of, one, the parents coming back and two, nice as I was, those kids are not easy; you will find out for yourself. Spirited, you could call them. And three, there was that white van following me all night—"

"White van?"

"Yes."

"*Bad* white van?"

"Yep."

"And what do you mean, kidf?" said Nosy.

"The kids in the car."

"Oh," said Nosy, who perhaps was not too bright. "Fo not the fame kids wot has just runned off and gone down that there hatch into the bowlf of the ship."

Pete turned round. It had been a long, long evening. He saw the car and the deck, empty, a hatch open. "Bowels," he said.

"Pardon?"

"Not bowls. Bowels. As in innards. We'll never find 'em now."

"No time," said Nosy. "Captain wantf to fee you."

"Never rains but it pours," said Nanny Pete.

5

"They'll never find us now," said Cassian.

Neither of his sisters answered. They did not approve of people stating the obvious. They kept climbing down the vertical ladder of greasy iron. It descended into a darkness that smelled of oil. From far below came weird clankings and rumblings and once what sounded like a voice howling. It was not an encouraging noise. Neither Primrose nor Daisy wished to find out what was making it. So they were most delighted when Cassian stepped off the ladder at a sort of landing. He switched on his pocket flashlight, clamped it between his teeth, and began to turn the locking wheel on a huge metal door. Pulling the door open a crack, he peeped out.

"Well?" hissed Daisy.

"All clear," hissed Cassian back.

The girls followed him through the door.

They were in a long corridor that stretched away as far as the eye could see in both directions. Underfoot was a soft, wine-red carpet with yellow piping at the edges. The walls were made of mahogany. From the ceiling hung cut-glass chandeliers. "Quite charming," said Primrose.

"Highly select. But where are we?" said Daisy.

Cassian, a keen student of shipbuilding, said, "Probably the first-class accommodation deck." He pointed down the left-hand wall, in which were set many doors. "Suites, I should think," he said.

"Marvelous," said Daisy. She grasped a brass doorknob and shoved open the door. "Well, I must say that this is really perfectly acceptable."

She was right.

The Darlings were standing in an enormous stateroom with gold-mounted sofas, a walnut dining table with six Chippendale chairs, and a grandfather clock. "Commence exploration procedure. Report back in five," said Daisy out of the corner of her mouth, shooting the large brass bolts on the door.

Five minutes later, the children were gathered, flushed and happy, on the sofa. "Bathroom," said Primrose. "Fizz bath, swirl bath, power shower, needle shower, washbasin, ivory toothbrushes provided. Hot water switched on."

"Check," said Daisy. "Cassian?"

"Three bedrooms," said Cassian. "Four-poster bunks, brocade bedspreads, reading lamps, voicetubes, and room service menus."

"How delightful," said Daisy. "And I have discovered a map."

The map was a large object, framed. It showed all the decks of the ship. Three of the decks were marked FOR THE ATTENTION OF OUR HONORED PASSENGERS. These showed the first-class cabins, ballroom, and dining accommodations. Another two decks were marked FOR THE ATTENTION OF PASSENGERS. These were the second-class and third-class cabins, small, windowless, and close to the propeller shaft and the crew lavatories. And another six decks, marked BENEATH THE ATTENTION OF PASSENGERS, showed the locations of the engine rooms, kitchens, laundries, livestock units, freezers, skate-sharpening workshops, bridge, and all the other facilities (it said on the map) installed on the *Kleptomanic* to give her passengers the Atlantic Crossing of a Lifetime—Luxurious, Efficient, Speedy (Six Days!).

"Engine rooms first," said Cassian.

"Kitchens next," said Primrose.

"But what," said Daisy, "if they catch us?"

"Judging by Nanny Pete," said Primrose, "they could not catch a cold."

"Not if they used both hands," said Cassian.

"Well, time to freshen up, and off we go," said Daisy.

She took a needle shower and a power-blast bath. Primrose jumped into the whirlpool and swam against the spin for a few minutes. Cassian wetted his hand and patted his hair a bit flatter. Refreshed, they set off.

This time, they noticed things.

The empty corridor outside the cabin had been empty for some time, judging by the puffs of dust their feet raised as they walked along it. The hair Cassian had left across the iron emergency door was unbroken; they had not been followed. The shaft was still dark and oily. The worrying clankings and churnings still rose from the darkness below, but the howling had stopped. "Must we?" said Daisy.

"I have got to do what I have got to do," said Cassian nobly. "You don't have to."

"All for one and one for all!" said Primrose.

Down they went; down, down into the heart of darkness, blackness illimitable. The noise of grinding and churning grew louder. "I say!" said Cassian. "How thrilling!"

"Mmm," said his sisters. Daisy would have quite liked to take Cassian's hand, and she suspected the same was true of Primrose. But you cannot hold hands on a vertical ladder, and besides, the nanny training (brave little men! whether you were boys or girls) stood in their way.

"We're here," said Cassian's voice from the darkness below. They stood on a metal deck. They saw the flashlight beam play on a steel door. They saw the wheel turn, the door open, light stream in, a ruddy light that flickered. They walked out of the shaft.

They were in a huge hall, with things like pillars rising from the middle of its floor. The light came from a grate in the bottom of one of the pillars, inside which an enormous fire was burning. Two men with shovels were digging coal from a great mound on the floor and hurling it into the fire. High in the shadows great beams and levers turned, slow and smooth.

"Fantastic," breathed Cassian.

"Ahem," said Daisy, in a strange, high voice.

For standing watching them were two giants. Both of them were two meters tall and carried huge, dripping oil cans. Both of them were as wide as houses. The one on the right was probably the bigger of the two. There was a handle on the back of his head, though Daisy could not imagine anyone strong enough to lift him.

Cassian smiled, the smile of someone completely at home. "Ah," he said. "The engine room."

"Actually, it's the stokehold," said the man without the handle.

"Thank you. And you are?"

"George," said the man without the handle. "And this is Giant Luggage."

"Hur, hur," said the man with the handle.

"Where's the chief?"

"There," said George, pointing to a glassed-in control room on the far side of the floor. "He won't see you, though."

"We'll see," said Cassian briskly. "Carry on oiling, men."

George gave him a sort of half salute. Giant Luggage said, "Hur, hur." They lumbered off into the shadows.

"Well done," said Primrose.

"Most effective," said Daisy.

"Huh?" said Cassian, and his sisters realized that they might as well have told a fish how clever it was to be such a good swimmer. "Let's see the chief."

The closer they went to the control room, the odder it seemed. It was basically a room attached to the side of the stokehold, with glass walls. But the glass walls had been painted black from the inside. Only a pair of clear patches remained. As they drew closer, they saw that the clear patches had eyes behind them—brown eyes, red-rimmed, rolling horribly. Above the clank and boom of machinery and the hiss of steam came a strange, worrying noise: the sound of dozens of clocks, chiming.

There was a door in the wall of the chief's shack. Beside it was a doorbell. Beside the bell was a label that read RING AND DIE.

"Perhaps we'll leave it," said Daisy.

But Cassian was approaching the bell, not with his thumb, but with a little gadget he had taken from his pocket. He touched the brass bell push. There was a crackle and a flash that for a second lit up the lofty vault of the stokehold, with its gantries and walkways and slow-turning cams. "Goodness me," said Cassian, reading a dial on the gadget. "Ten thousand volts. How very impressive."

"Just as well you didn't put your thumb on it," said Primrose.

"Do me a favor," said Cassian.

"Sorry."

The door opened as far as its three chains would allow. A face appeared in the crack. It had a long chin and blubbery red lips, with eyes to match. "You're alive," it said.

"Of course," said Cassian. "We would like some information, if you please—"

"Go away!" howled the chief, mopping his eyes with a filthy handkerchief.

"Perhaps we should come back when you are feeling better," said Daisy.

"Noooobody loves me!" howled the chief.

"Frankly," said Daisy, "I am not surprised."

"Yowooooo!" howled the chief. The door slammed shut. There was the sound of dozens of bolts sliding home.

"That's the chief, then," said Cassian.

"No manners," said Daisy. But she said it slowly.

For her mind was not on that figure whose face had hung tearstained in the door crack. She was thinking about what she had glimpsed past him, in that weird black-walled room.

The walls had been covered in clocks: cuckoo clocks, grandfather clocks, ships' chronometers. In the middle of the clocks was an elaborate glass case, its top rising in a sort of pyramid to a gilt crown, the crown itself surmounted by the gilt figure of an eagle, but an eagle with four necks and four heads. And in the case, staring out at the world with mournful eyes of amber glass, the head of a teddy bear. Only Daisy could have seen it, absorbed it in a lightning flash of her huge mind. . . .

"Did you see that bear's head?" said Primrose. "Bit odd, I thought."

"Chief engineers are often slightly eccentric," said Cassian.

"Everybody knows that," said Daisy. "Come this way."

"Where are we going?" said Primrose.

"Wait and see," said Daisy, pursing her lips. She had no idea, of course. But she had been brought up by nannies, and nannies are never, ever wrong.

First, there was a deck full of machines that Cassian said were generators. "Up, up," cried Daisy, thrusting open a door. Beyond the door were corridors and more corridors, the smell of cooking, which was tempting, and the sound of voices yelling, which was not. Actually, all three Darlings were beginning to feel extremely tired and absolutely starving. "It is way past our bedtime," said Daisy.

Then, somehow, they were standing by a railing, looking

down. Far below was the gleam of polished wood and some-thing like a stage. Daisy said, in a breathless sort of voice, "The ballroom! How lovely!" The sound of a piano floated up from below, a jazzy, bluesy tune, happy and sad at the same time. The playing stopped. The figure of a woman in a red velvet ball gown floated across the ballroom floor and was gone.

The little Darlings stood with their chins on the railing, watching the emptiness below. They were away from home, without Nanny, Papa, or Secretary Mummy. It was way past their bedtime. They should have felt as empty as the ball-room.

But when you have been brought up by nannies, you learn that having each other is enough. There was only one kind of emptiness they were feeling.

"I'm starving," said Primrose.

"Where are those kitchens?" said Cassian.

"They'll be down there, so the waiters can bring delicious food to the ladies in the lovely dresses in between dances with charming men in tailcoats," said Daisy.

"Swoony trollop," said Cassian, and started marching downstairs.

The ballroom was fearsomely dusty, except for the grand piano on the stage, which gleamed, as if polished frequently. In the back regions beside a bar was a cupboard in the wall, with two buttons next to it. One of the buttons read KITCHEN.

"It's a dumbwaiter," said Cassian. "Hop in." Primrose hopped.

"No," said Daisy.

Voices sounded at the other end of the ballroom. They were gruff and over-excited. "Thisaway!" they cried. "Look! Tracks!"

"It's probably not us they're looking for," said Daisy. "They didn't seem to mind us in the stokehold."

"D'you want to find out?" said Cassian, leaping into the dumbwaiter.

Daisy pointed her toes and swung her legs elegantly in after him. Cassian stuck his frowning black head out and pressed the KITCHEN button. Down they went into the dark, Daisy clutching Primrose's hand, though Primrose seemed quite calm, which probably had something to do with being close to a kitchen.

The lift came to a halt. Through its open front, they were looking between endless rows of black cast-iron stoves. Between the stoves was a bottom the size of an elephant's, dressed in gigantic black-and-white-checked chef's trousers. Above the bottom was a white jacket, filled with fat the way a sausage skin is filled with sausage. On top of all this was a tiny head with ears like fungi, on which was balanced a tall, thin chef's hat. One of the arms seemed to be throwing a ladle at somebody. "They're not *here*!" a voice was yelling, in a sort of thick squeak. "I haven't *seen* any children! I've looked *everywhere*! Now get out of my *kitchen*—!"

"Galley," said a timid voice.

"*Shut up, shut up*, because I've worked my fingers to the *bone* and now I'm off to *bed!*"

"They're looking for us, all right," said Daisy.

The chef picked up a roast chicken and waddled off, gnawing. The lights went out. Cassian tiptoed out of the dumbwaiter and turned them on again.

"Steak and kidney pies," said Primrose, lifting a pot lid and sniffing. "Baked beans. Warm white bread. Chips. Get some plates."

There was then a long silence, broken only by the clash of knives and forks. Nannies did not hold with pies, chips, beans, or any bread except brown yuck that tasted like cardboard. This was a fantastic treat. And it was hard to think that anyone who could eat food this delicious could really be dangerous.

Daisy finished her second plateful. "Tired," she said.

"Back to the cabin," said Cassian.

"Suite," said Daisy.

"Thank you, dear," said Cassian.

Primrose merely yawned.

They washed up, procured some bread and eggs for breakfast, climbed back into the dumbwaiter, and pressed a button that read CABINS. As they went past the ballroom, the lift filled with piano music. There was a brief glimpse of a figure in a red velvet dress on the stage; then the darkness again, then a corridor lined with doors, lit by small yellow lights stretching away as far as the eye could see. Daisy scowled at the map and took them up shafts and round corners and into the empty land, where the wine-red carpets were frosted gray with dust. Here they found their suite and slept like logs.

Next morning, early, Primrose cooked an excellent breakfast of fried bread and stolen eggs over a small fire Cassian made in the stateroom grate from a couple of chairs. It felt quite homelike, once you got used to it. After breakfast, they had fizz baths and explosion spa showers and got dressed. Daisy was wearing a pensive frown. She said, "We've got to do something."

"About what?"

"Secretary Mummy and Papa."

"What about them?"

"Somebody ought to see if they're all right."

Her brother and sister shrugged. "If you want."

"So," said Daisy. "We'd better find out who runs the place round here."

"The captain," said Cassian.

"There won't be a captain on a messed-up ship like this," said Primrose.

"Bet there will," said Cassian.

"But will he be a person of goodwill?" said Daisy.

There was a silence. Everyone saw what she meant.

"We could have a look round," said Daisy.

"Case the joint," said Primrose.

"See how it all works," said Cassian.

"And Secretary Mummy won't even notice we're not there," said Daisy.

"Nor will Papa," said Primrose.

There was a silence as this gloomy truth sank in. "Well," said Daisy eventually. "We can't sit here moping all day. Off we go."

Off they went.

They started in the engine room again. The giant with the handle on his head raised a paw and said, "Hur, hur," with an expression on his face that might have been a grin. This was encouraging. The chief engineer's eyes were still whirling in his spy holes, in time to a weird tintinnabulation of clocks. This was not encouraging. The girls removed Cassian from the fascinating generator rooms by threats of violence and marched down the trail of delicious smells that led to the kitchens. This time they did not use the dumbwaiter, but walked over the deep carpets of an empty dining saloon with long mahogany tables laid with gleaming silver and bright glasses. There was a serving door with round portholes. From behind the door came shouting and the clank of pans. Primrose made a beeline for it.

"Wait," said Cassian. "Where are you going?"

"Aren't you hungry?" said Primrose.

"Well, yes, of course," said Cassian.

"But there are burglars after us," said Daisy. "It is not wise."

"Wise, schmise," said Primrose out of the side of her sweet pink mouth. "A chef loves a compliment." She marched forward, shoved open the doors, and stepped into the kitchen.

The ceiling was low, the heat intense. Cast-iron stoves stretched into the distance. Scurrying figures came and went behind rolling banks of steam. Primrose marched straight into the nearest steam bank, became hazy, and vanished. Daisy and Cassian were beginning to follow when a huge voice boomed out of the fog. *"What,"* it roared, *"are you doing in my keetchen?"*

The fog rolled away. Primrose was standing with her thin white hands on her pink gingham hips, her head thrown back, looking into a vast, lard-white face. On top of the face was a chef's hat the size of a pillowcase. Below the face was a white coat and a pair of enormous check trousers, both filled to bursting. In the middle of the face were two little black eyes, a button nose, and a rosebud mouth, from which the voice was booming.

"Relax, Chef," said Primrose. "My brother and sister and I wished to say that not finding you here last night, we took a little dinner—"

"*Three pie!*" roared Chef. "Eight slice bread! Six thousand and twelve bean! Also egg, bacon, tomato—"

"We would have asked, of course," said Primrose, bending the truth with great casualness. "But there was no one here. And of course we—"

"*Food thiefs!*" bellowed Chef.

"But now we have owned up. And apologized. It is," said Primrose, "a fair cop, Chef."

"Ah." The chef looked nonplussed.

"And we wanted in addition and on top," said Primrose, "to present our compliments. You do an exquisitely baked bean. Also a very light touch with suet. I know my brother and sister agree. Not so, Daisy? Cassian?"

Daisy and Cassian said firmly, as they had been taught by their nannies, "Yes," and, "Aye," and, "Excellent." And watched in astonishment as this mountainous chef shifted his feet and looked at the floor and simpered and actually blushed.

"Well," said Chef, in a new, smaller voice. "Maybe you hungry, eh? We have here, let me see, leetle fillet shteak with onion smother and kartoffel dauphinoise; any good to you?"

"Sure is," said Primrose, slapping him on the back. Minions arrived with heaped-up plates. The children fell on the delicious viands at a table in the corner while the chef, cooking all the while in huge iron pans, chatted amiably about Great Sausages he had known. Having topped off a mighty elevenses with apple dumplings and ice cream buried under Alps of whipped cream, the children made an appointment for lunch and prepared to resume their explorations.

At this point a voice in the mists said, "Ahem."

A figure stepped into a patch of clear air.

The uniform was gone. Instead, there was a striped jersey, blue trousers, and army boots. But the face, large-chinned and heavy-browed, was unquestionably that of Pete, alias Nanny Petronella Fryer.

"You and me," said Nanny Pete, "have a duty to perform. We are off to see the captain."

"Gulp," said Daisy.

Two more burglars strolled out of the steam, their big hands hooked into their wide leather belts. They fell in behind, cutting off all possibility of escape.

"If you would be so good as to sleepy me?" said Pete.

"I beg your pardon?"

"Sleepy Hollow, follow."

"Ah."

They climbed stairs and went down corridors and side decks, miles of them. After ten minutes, they were on the green landing strip where the Jag was parked. In front of it was a building like a castle made of steel, with an elaborate door painted navy blue and decorated with gold anchors. In the middle, a design in gilt ropework and butterflies read CAPTAIN.

Pete opened the door and walked in. The children followed him. "Sit down," said Pete. Daisy sat down. The nanny burglar's face was closed. Daisy began to think that perhaps it would have been better not to have stowed away in the Jaguar.

Too late now. "Chin up," she said.

"Obviously," said Cassian.

"Natch," said Primrose, adjusting her Alice band.

They began to look around them.

They were in a long room, with windows all down the opposite side to the door. There was a steering wheel in the middle, with a compass in front of it. The compass was made of brass. There was a pink frill round it. There were matching frills on the engine room telegraphs beside it and a huge vase of pink roses on the chart table. Beyond the windows, the gigantic offices of the Transglobal Steamship Company frowned over the pointed bows of the ship.

Cassian was scowling darkly. He had never been on a ship's bridge before, but he was pretty sure that normal bridges would not be this frilly.

Suddenly, a red telephone started ringing. Nanny Pete started toward it. But before he was halfway, Daisy had picked it up. "Hellay?" said a voice on the other end. "Hellay?"

Daisy said, "Hello." Nanny Pete had stopped in mid-stride. Agonized suspense furrowed his brow.

"Is this AAA Aardvark Child Minding and Security?" said the voice, which sounded like a horse gargling with cut glass.

"At your service, madam," said Daisy, sliding smoothly into nanny mode.

"I need someone immediately," said the voice. "Honestly, I'm at my wits' end."

"What have they done this time?" said Daisy soothingly.

"Dropped a ball," said the voice. "A tennis ball. On the carpet. And who's going to pick it up, I'd like to know?"

"Who am I speaking to?"

"Lady Orthodonta Strimlingham," said the voice, now sounding like a horse close to tears. "All the servants have gone and now Nanny and there's this ball just . . . lying here."

"Give me your number," said Daisy. "We'll call you right back."

"Oh, thank you, thank you!" said the voice. "But do hurry!"

Daisy hung up and scribbled the number on a pad of scented pink paper tied with a ribbon to the steering wheel. Nanny Pete was staring at her, shaking his head in astonishment. "Respect," he said. "Nice one."

"Oh, I don't know," said Daisy, pleased despite herself.

"What now?" said Cassian. His mind was full of mighty cylinders, colossal steering gear, titanic generators, bunkers filled with mountains of coal, and lakes of sticky black oil. He hated all these frills.

"Well, quite," said a voice from the other end of the bridge. "What, indeed?"

All three children spun round. Nanny Pete knuckled his forehead respectfully. In a doorway stood a tall woman with black hair and dark glasses. She was wearing a crimson velvet dressing gown. Daisy noticed that her toenails were beautifully painted.

"We are Daisy, Cassian, and Primrose," said Daisy politely. "And who, may I ask, are you?"

The woman gazed upon them for a worryingly long time. "I'm the captain," she said.

"You can't be," said Cassian, horrified.

"Of course she can," said both his sisters together.

The lady yawned. She was very tall, and her scent was like a spring garden, and her makeup was impeccable. "But what are you doing on my ship?"

"We stowed away with Nanny Pete here," said Daisy. Nanny Pete blushed tomato red and looked at his boots. "We quite like it here. But we think we ought to tell our parents. They fret if they're on their own, you know. Well, Papa might, anyway."

The captain pulled down her dark glasses and studied Daisy with great interest. "You think so?"

"Probably not, actually," said Daisy gloomily. It was sometimes possible to have fantasies about being loved and wanted, but they never seemed to last. She took refuge in efficiency. "Oh, by the way. There was a telephone call." Conscientiously, Daisy told the captain about Lady Strimlingham and the ball horror.

"Excellent." The captain picked up the phone and dialed. There was a distant yammering. "An operative will be with you directly, my lady," she cooed, and hung up. "Pete, duty nanny to the Jag deck."

"Aye, aye," said Pete.

"Now then, children," said the captain. "Your parents. I honestly think you'd better go straight back to them."

"Last thing we want," said Cassian. "We like it here."

"And of course Nanny Pete stole a whole lot of stuff," said Daisy sweetly. "And we might tell someone."

"Plus the food at home is absolutely awful," said Primrose.

"Was," said the captain.

"I beg your pardon?"

"You saw a white van," said the captain.

"How did you know?" said Cassian.

"Psychic," said the captain, looking grim. "When I said back to your parents, I meant back to your parents, not back home. I shouldn't think there's much of home left. But if you don't want to go, you don't want to go. So," she said, beaming, as if the bright side of something had suddenly occurred to her. "Welcome aboard. But you'll have to work your passage."

"Work?" said Daisy.

"My spies tell me Primrose is an enthusiastic and skillful cook," said the captain.

"Does a bear go to the lavatory in the woods?" said Primrose mildly.

"And that Cassian has . . . engineering talents."

"'Spose," said Cassian.

"And that you yourself . . . Daisy, is it not? . . . have watched nannies in action."

"Closely, and with great vigilance."

"Too right," said Pete.

"Well, then." A small, unshaven nanny trotted onto the bridge. "Ah, Fingers. Are you duty nanny?"

"Yes'm." Fingers giggled and bit off a chew of tobacco from an evil-looking black plug. "Awright, kids?" He held out a bag. "Gobstoppers," he said. "Go on, have two. 'Scuse me, gotta spit." Fingers went outside.

The captain pressed a button with a long red fingernail. "Jag crew, prepare launchpad," she said.

"Are you serious?" said Daisy.

The captain looked hard at Daisy. "Is there a problem?"

"Well," said Daisy. "It was just that he didn't seem, well, all that nannyish."

The captain seemed shocked. "What was wrong?"

"Chewing tobacco," said Daisy.

"Spitting," said Primrose.

"Gobstoppers," said Cassian.

"And some of the things Nanny Pete did were actually *kind,*" said Primrose. "So we knew there was something odd going on straightaway."

"Though he was very good at not getting hurt," said Daisy, in fairness. "Exceptionally good, really."

"Ah," said the captain, looking at Nanny Pete, who was shifting from foot to foot in the background. "Pete, you may go." She filed her nails as Pete made a sharp exit. "Well, of course, our people have been trained in Wormwood Scrubs and Sing Sing, not the Nanny Academy." She paused. "So you're nanny experts, eh?"

"We've had eighteen," said Primrose with simple pride.

"Nineteen," said Cassian.

"The last one didn't count."

"And now," said Daisy, "I think we should ring up Papa and tell him that we are unavoidably detained in a safe place."

"By all means," said the captain.

But there was only the answering machine. "Mr. and Mrs. Darling are in the Caribbean," it said. "Please leave your invitation after the tone. Bing bong."

"Hello," said Daisy. "We are away with our new nanny. See you sometime." She put down the receiver. "You heard that?"

"Yup," said her brother and sister. There was a gloomy

silence. It is nice to be cared about by your parents, even if you hardly know them.

Outside the bridge, Nanny Fingers spat more tobacco juice, climbed into the Jag, waved to the Darlings, and was swung over the side. They watched from the bridge as the black car beetled down the quay and out of the dock gate.

The captain gave them a dazzling smile. "Lunch, anyone?" she said, brightly. "I'll get Chef to rustle something up."

It was yet another amazing repast, consisting of tomato soup, shrimp burgers, pancakes with maple syrup, and four kinds of juice, each more delicious than the last. The Darling children ate deeply, then leaned back in their chairs. "Excellent," said Daisy. Frankly, the notion of meeting this Captain of Burglars had been a daunting one. But she seemed to be turning out to be as nice as she was beautiful.

"I know it's not like being at home," said the captain, "but in our simple way we try, we try."

"Burnt porridge is what we get at home," said Cassian.

"Well," said Daisy. "Back to the suite, I think."

"One moment," said the captain. "Daisy, would you do me a favor? A word, perhaps?" She walked to a bank of voice pipes, blew into one of them, and said, "Nanny Pete to bridge, chop, chop."

The captain led Daisy into a small boudoir decorated with framed watercolors of famous crime scenes and a large bunch of freesias. "Sit down," she said. "Drink?"

"Bit early for me," said Daisy.

"Ah," said the captain. "Quite. Now, dear . . . what were your brother and sister called again, by the way?"

"I'm Daisy," said Daisy. "And they're Primrose and Cassian."

The captain poured a small glass of clear liquid from a decanter and downed it at a gulp. "Yes," she said, her beautiful features for a moment distant and pensive. "Quite so, quite so. Well, the question is, er . . . Daisy, what are we to do with you? You cannot simply . . . be here."

"Suppose you explain what 'here' is," said Daisy. "Then perhaps we can come up with a plan."

"Excellent idea," said the captain. She pulled a silken cord, and a curtain swished back from a whiteboard. "We have as you know, er, pinched the SS *Kleptomanic*—"

"Which is still here," said Daisy.

"Bear with me," said the captain, a pained smile flitting over her scarlet lips. "On the *Kleptomanic* are two hundred and ninety-three burglars, first-floor men, cat operatives, ram raiders, and allied trades. Some of the worst and most incompetent burglars, if I may for a moment blow our trumpet, that crime has ever seen. But a very nice type of burglar. Not the kind of burglar at home in the urban jungle. The kind of burglar at home in an older, more forgiving world. Who prefers jewelery and antique paintings to DVD recorders, whatever they are. The kind of burglar who wishes to burgle his way to the quiet life. It is my plan one day to sail away with my burglars to that quiet life or, anyway, somewhere where their special talents will come in handy."

"So why haven't you already gone?"

The captain uncapped a felt-tip pen and wrote on the whiteboard the words *lack of funds*. She began to write something else, changed her mind, and put the top back on the pen.

"Funds?"

"Money."

"Ah." Daisy nodded politely.

"But do not worry your head about this," said the captain. "What we aim to do on the *Kleptomanic* is improve skills and develop, ahem, other sources of income. And this is where you come in."

"Me?"

"Yes, you," said the captain. "Ah, Nanny Pete! Enter!"

And into the room sidled Nanny Pete, looking kindly, tough, and a little flustered. Behind him came Primrose and Cassian.

"Pete," said the captain. "Daisy here is on the nanny project. And if it is all right with them, we'll attach Primrose to the galley and Cassian to the engine room. Would that suit, do you think?"

"Down to the ground," said Daisy. "But what is it you want me to do?"

"Observe our nannies in action," said the captain. "And having observed, make recommendations and report to me. With your experience of the nanny world, your views will be of the greatest help. I am having rather a busy time just now—"

"The Edward," said Pete. "White Van Dan."

"I beg your pardon?" said Daisy.

"Nothing," said the captain firmly, frowning at Pete, who blushed to the roots of his tattoo.

"Dear me, you do look peaky. A junior aspirin, Pete, and off to bed with you!" said Daisy, pursing her lips.

"Perfect!" cried the captain, ushering her out of the door. "Total nanny! Now run along and get a uniform and Pete will introduce you to the key burglars and you can get settled in. Now, is everybody sure they are happy?"

"Lots of machinery," said Cassian gruffly. "Nice."

"And it's all sorely in need of a service!" cried the captain.

"Working by the side of Chef!" cried Primrose. "Such a sweet person! Such an artist of the spoon and saucepan!"

"Hmm," said the captain. "So off you go. Excellent. Excellent!"

In a huge walk-in wardrobe of nanny gear, Pete Fryer found Daisy a brown bowler hat, a greenish uniform that fitted pretty well, an apron, a pair of brogues, and a notebook. She spent the rest of the day exploring. At suppertime, she saw Nanny Fingers being helped down the ship's main stairs on his way back from his nanny mission. There were scorch marks all over him. "They tied him up and ironed him," said Pete Fryer. "Little perishers."

"What did he expect?" said Daisy, sighing.

A couple of days passed in the purest enjoyment. Then a bell shrilled, and the loudspeaker said, "Sub-nanny Daisy to bridge, in uniform."

With a beating heart Daisy donned overall, apron, bowler,

and brogues and put her notebook in her pocket. Pete Fryer knocked on the suite door. "I'll see you up to the windy," he said.

"I beg your pardon?"

"Windy ridge, bridge. Come on now."

On the way up the stairs, Daisy took off her nail varnish, though Pete said there was no need. (Daisy made a note.) Nanny Huggins was duty nanny—a small, scrawny burglar, just about clean shaven, with a kind smile that showed a gold tooth. (Daisy made a note.) "The Marchesa di Costaplenti. Interesting client. Would you mind going along as sub-nanny and observer?" said the captain, who today was wearing a sharply tailored suit with a pencil skirt.

"I should be delighted," said Daisy.

The Jag swung down. Nanny Huggins drove at top speed out of the docks, through the Old Town, and into Happy Valley, where the big houses were. As the Jag shot past, a builder stopped digging a hole, straightened up, and made a rapid call on a mobile phone.

The di Costaplenti house was huge and pink and more or less invisible from the road. Huggins stopped the Jag in a yellow fan of expensive gravel. (Daisy made a note.) Huggins jumped out, ran up the steps to the front door, and walloped on the panels with her bowler hat. A butler opened up. "Hello, big boy," said Huggins. "We're the new nannies." (Daisy made a note.)

"I will inform her ladyship," said the butler, looking down his nose. "She has asked that you commence your duties immediately. She does not require to meet you. The servants' entrance is round the back; you can't miss it, just look for the dustbins. The nursery wing is adjacent." A watery smile played on his lips. "And may God have mercy on your souls."

"Very nice," said Huggins, rubbernecking as they marched round the back of the house. "Solid gold door knocker, don't see many of them nowadays, incitement to crime, really. Oh, look, some poor child has left his sweet liddle teddy bear—" He bent down to pick up the charming animal, stretched out his hand—

"Nooooo!" cried Daisy, grabbing hold of Nanny Huggins's green elasticated belt and yanking him back.

Huggins looked puzzled. "But it's a dear little stuffed koala," he said.

"Ha!" said Daisy scornfully. She cut a bamboo from a nearby clump and gave the koala a good jab. As soon as the stuffed Australian moved a fraction of a millimeter, a huge pair of steel jaws leaped out of the dead leaves and came together with a dreadful clang, cutting the bamboo clean in half.

"The old Killer Koala trick," said Daisy, writing in her notebook. "You were saying?"

A new, hard light glinted in Huggins's eye. "Nothing," he said.

Daisy picked up the koala shreds and walked through the cloud of flies over the dustbins scattered around the servants' entrance. Huggins came after her, trying to look as if he was not hanging back.

Rollo and Pandora di Costaplenti were dressed in matching green velvet suits, with buckle shoes. Their nursery wing was horribly tidy. "Well!" cried Nanny Huggins, who had recovered her composure. "What shall we do today?"

"Wanna go roller blading," said Rollo.

"Indoors," said Pandora.

"Lovely idea!" cried Nanny Huggins. (Daisy wrote in her book.) "Wait here, Nanny Daise." She sidled off into the house.

Daisy had to admit that Rollo and Pandora had excellent technique. Once they had got the roller blades on their little feet, they hauled ice hockey sticks down from the walls and began to play at an exceptionally high level of violence. They smashed the chandelier, two of the windows, and all the Peter Rabbit crockery in the kitchenette. Then they started fighting. Daisy finished the note she was making in her book and stepped between them. An ice hockey stick smote her on the head, but the hats worn by nannies are built by the same company that makes hats for motorcycle racing. So she only staggered a little, took a deep breath, and cried, *"Stop it!"*

Actually, the word *cried* does not even half describe the sound that came out of her mouth. It was so loud that it cracked one of the few unbroken windows in the children's wing. Rollo and Pandora stared at her, white-faced. "Now then, children," said Sub-nanny Daisy. "Let's not be rough and naughty."

Rollo's face took on an unpleasant twist. He opened his mouth to curse her.

Sub-nanny Daisy had been brought up by nannies and knew exactly what to do. "Into the bathroom!" she cried, gripping his ear with the Nanny Earlock and swinging him off his feet. "Wash out his nasty mouth with soap and water, not that nice scented soap, no, this nasty yellow soap, rubadubadubadub!"

"Groo!" cried Rollo. "Arghblblblbl!" His pasty face disappeared behind a cloud of bubbles.

"We'll be good!" shrieked Pandora. "Weally, weally, weally good!"

"That's as may be," said Sub-nanny Daisy, sniffing. "Now off we go to bed with no supper."

"Oh, Nana!" bubbled Rollo.

"Unfair!" moaned Pandora.

"Quick march!" snapped Daisy. "Go!"

Whimpering, they went.

Daisy tucked them up and read them a story. They fell asleep, good as gold. Daisy tiptoed out of the bedroom, shooting the bolts behind her. There was no sign of Nanny Huggins in the nursery wing. So Daisy pushed open the green baize door and went into the house.

She found it pretty ordinary. The marble floors were normal marble floors, and the chandeliers glittered away very much as expected. The usual pictures of chilly ladies hung on the walls, and the carpets lapped over the ankles in an unsurprising manner. A few servants skulked here and there, not paying any attention to each other. The sound of breaking glass and sea shanties came from the butler's pantry. "Ho, hum," said Daisy to herself, and headed for the dining room.

And sure enough, there was Nanny Huggins, up to his elbows in spoons.

Nanny Huggins jumped slightly, clanking his swag bag. "Oh, it's you," he said.

"It is indeed I," said Daisy, smoothing her apron.

"So do me a favor," said Huggins. "Have a look round and see if you can find—" he took a scrap of paper out of his pocket—". . . a portion of bear."

"A bear?"

Huggins's lips moved soundlessly as he read. "'Yur," he said. "On a . . . diagonal . . ."

"Mahogany?"

"What I said, mahogany—er, shield."

"Very good," said Daisy, and scooted off. Frowning.

There were long galleries; short galleries; saloons; coal, wine, and root cellars; and a basement containing a cricket net and a medium-sized theater. A small door in the side wall of the theater said TROPHY ROOM. Daisy strode up to it, pushed it open, and stopped dead. She nearly said, *"Eek!"* But since she was in nanny uniform, she merely said, "My goodness!"

She was staring at a tiger.

She counted to ten, then gave a little sigh. Of course it was only a stuffed tiger. All around it were other animals, bravely shot at extreme range by the Marchese di Costaplenti, stuffed, and mounted on shields. There was an elephant's head. There was a pygmy shrew. And high on the wall was something that looked like an anteater's nose, made of worn, brownish plush. A brass plate underneath it read LEFT LEG OF THE ROYAL EDWARD, LORP TOMBOLA, YEAR OF THE RAT.

Ignoring the hundreds of glass eyes gazing beadily upon her from the walls, Daisy climbed onto a stool, unhooked the left leg and its shield, and returned to the dining room.

She and Nanny Huggins dragged the swag bags back to the nursery wing. The children were still being as good as gold, or anyway their bedroom door was still bolted and there was no sign of a tunnel.

"How did you do it?" said Huggins.

Daisy told him.

"Poor little devils," said Huggins.

"They'll be grateful later," said Daisy. "Now tell me, what do you know about the Royal Edward, the Lorp, and tombolas?"

"Wha?" said Huggins, jaw swinging.

"Very little, I see," said Daisy. "Are you going to stand there all day, or are we going to get out of here?"

"Sorry," said Huggins.

A lugging of swag bags. A screech of Jaguar tires, Huggins's brown bowler low over the wheel. Behind them, something huge and white coming into the road. A flop of ramps. A digger, a dozer, a dumper roaring into the di Costaplenti drive. A huge cloud of dust rising in the still, blue air . . .

Then they were round the corner.

Daisy made a note and put the book away.

Back at the ship, there was the captain, wearing a tight black satin dress slit to the hip. "Well?" she said.

"Got some loot," said Huggins.

"And Sub-nanny Daisy?"

"Perfectly acceptable," said Daisy.

"Nah," said Nanny Huggins, head hanging. "Captain, I cannot tell a lie. Was it not having been for Sub-nanny—no!—Senior Nanny Daisy, I shudder to think what would have happened." He did indeed shudder. Daisy knew he was thinking of the Killer Koala.

The captain raised a perfect eyebrow.

"Too true, one fears," said Daisy.

The captain pressed a large pink button. "Mug of cocoa," she said. "Then debrief."

"Then what?" said Daisy, who had questions of her own.

"It is like this," said the captain. "My dear burglars are . . . well, perhaps a little softhearted. In childhood, many of them were very close to their parents. There are things about life that only someone who has been brought up by nannies can explain. And explain someone must, before one of our boys gets hurt. Do you get my drift?"

"Of course," said Daisy. "You would like me to make a small speech."

"Indeed."

A klaxon was sounding in the bowels of the ship. A steward arrived with a mug of cocoa on a silver salver. Daisy drank, extending her little finger. Far in the distance was a muffled clanging and thundering, like the sound of big boots on iron ladders. A loudspeaker on the wall said, "Five-minute call for Captain and Nanny Daisy."

"Frightfully good cocoa," said Daisy.

"Your sister made it," said the captain. "She tells me the secret is to put the merest suspicion of whiskey in it. Now drink up and come along, darling." She led Daisy to an area of the ship she had not previously visited, down huge, lyre-shaped stairs to a round landing crusted with gold. "In here," she said. And suddenly they were in dusty corridors slung with cables, full of a sound like the sea breaking on rocks.

"We're on!" said the captain. She swished onto a huge deck, surrounded by red velvet curtains. Daisy stood dazzled by lights.

It was a stage. Beyond the lights was a sea of burglars. Daisy stood in her nanny uniform, hands folded, trying not to look surprised. "Ladies and gentlemen, cullies and nannies," cried the captain. "I have the honor of presenting . . . Nanny Daisy!"

There was a roar of applause. Obviously Huggins had been spreading the word. Daisy kept her hands folded and was annoyed to feel her cheeks go pink. The captain swept aside, hand out, bowing. Daisy stepped up to the lectern.

"Ahem," she said. "These remarks will, I hope, be of use to one and all. AAA Aardvark caters for a most exclusive type of parent, too rich to show affection to their children, too busy to remember their names. The children are remorseless and clever. One must be continually on guard against the little brutes, displaying no chink in the nanny armor. During the recent assignment, I took notes. I thought they might come in useful for those seeking hints on correct nanny deportment." She opened her notebook. "So here we go. On stopping the nanny mobile outside the client's house, gravel was blasted everywhere, which was very nice but not nanny behavior. Nanny Huggins has a nice smile, but it shows teeth. The correct nanny is at all times saying, 'Prune,' and, 'Prism,' and never shows amusement or"—Daisy looked up—"gold teeth."

There was a murmur, with nervous grinning and a discreet xylophonic tooth tapping.

"Next," said Daisy, "we come to the Killer Koala. Never,

never touch a toy until you have made a detailed check for cables, trip wires, laser beams, and other trigger devices."

"It was a sweet little teddy," said Nanny Huggins from the audience.

"The sweeter the bait, the sharper the hook," said Daisy. "How many fingers have you got?"

There was a short pause for counting. Then, "Ten," said Huggins.

"And how many would you have had if you had picked up that teddy?"

Silence.

"And as for roller blading indoors," said Daisy, "well! Can anyone tell me one thing in its favor?"

"Great," said a voice in the front row. "Fun, like."

"Fun!" said Daisy, in a voice that had a bad smell under its nose. "Oh. I see. And how many things can you tell me against it?"

There was a puzzled silence. Finally, a voice in the dark said, "Might bump your head?"

"Might—bump—your—head," said Daisy, in a voice whose nose now had icicles on it. "Well, it may interest you to know that nannies recognize four excellent reasons for not playing this rowdy and stupid game."

"Four?" said a voice.

The captain nodded, smiling brightly. "That's what the nanny said."

"One," said Daisy, "little ladies do not play rough games."

The captain smiled.

"Two," said Daisy, "little gentlemen are never rough with little ladies."

The captain beamed.

"Three," said Daisy, "roller skates, whether side by side or in-line, are a modern horror. The only suitable place for skating is a private ice rink with a membership of the nicest type."

"How very true!" cried the captain.

"Four," said Daisy, "and worst: All games are bad if they are rough; that goes without saying. But the worst games of all are games that force young ladies to show their *L*s."

"*L*s?" said a voice.

"Ahem!" said the captain discreetly, from behind the red velvet curtain into whose shelter she had backed. "I think Nanny Daisy is referring to . . . dread word . . . *legs!*"

"Aieeee!" shrieked Nanny Daisy, toppling sideways in a dead faint.

Cassian and Primrose jumped out of the audience and onto the stage and dragged their sister into the wings. Once out of sight of the audience, Daisy stood up. "Was I all right?" she said.

"Bit over the top," said Cassian. There were streaks of oil on his face.

"Why did you do it?" cried Primrose, who had flour in her hair. "They hated it!"

"Because if they're going to dress up as nannies, they'll have to behave like nannies," said Daisy. "Or they'll get caught. And hurt," she said, shuddering at the memory of the Killer Koala.

There was a silence. "How can they be so stupid?" said Primrose.

"Because they love children," said the captain's voice behind them. "They think that bad parents are creeps who deserve anything they get. But they think that bad children are really sweet and kind and have just gone astray and can be brought back to their senses with kindness. That's why Pete bought you takeaways and sang you bedtime songs."

There was a pause as this shocking idea sank in.

"Weird!" said Cassian.

"Half-baked!" said Primrose.

"Naïve!" said Daisy. "Lesson one at the Nanny Academy teaches nannies that all children are evil, wicked, mean, and nasty."

"So evil, wicked, mean, and nasty is what they get," said Cassian.

"It would be unkind to disappoint them," said Primrose.

"Actively rude," said Daisy.

"Hostile, even," said Cassian.

"I see," said the captain. "Come up to the bridge."

On the bridge, they sat on a chintz helmsman's suite. Daisy thought the captain looked sad. "Cheer up," Daisy said brightly. "We were all children once, you know. Things get better."

The captain filed a long red nail, shaking her head sadly. "It's not that," she said.

"So what is it?" said Cassian. He had spent all day regrinding a condenser valve, just one of the fantastic things there were to do in the *Kleptomanic*'s engine room. The shadow on the captain's lovely face was an astonishment to him. How could anyone be unhappy in this paradise of oil and steel?

"You don't want to know," said the captain.

"We certainly do," said Primrose. She had spent all day perfecting a recipe for Action Buns, whose ingredients included treacle, gin, and essence of greyhound. She was as much in her element as a croissant in an oven.

Daisy said, "You are hiding something from us For Our Own Good." The captain concentrated extra hard on her nail. "But we can look after ourselves, thank you very much."

"You are children," said the captain.

"What difference does that make?" said Daisy.

"We resent the imputation," said Primrose.

"Scandalous," said Cassian.

"And," said Daisy, "you can be quite sure that we know about the Royal Edward and"—here she groped a little in her mind, seeking half-heard remarks and half-glimpsed traffic items—"white vans."

Primrose was staring at her with her mild blue eyes. "Royal Edward," she said in a faint, puzzled voice. "Sure do."

Cassian was scowling at her under oily brows. "White vans?" he said, in tones whose bemusement only Daisy could hear. "Absolutely."

"And we want the full official story," said Daisy.

The captain sighed. "It's a fair cop," she said. "What should I tell you?"

"Everything," said Daisy. "Why you dress up as nannies. The lot."

"Starting from the top," said Primrose.

"Omitting nothing," said Cassian.

The captain sighed again and glanced at her jeweled Bulgari watch. "Very well," she said. "I have a few moments. But afterward, I am going to ask you some favors, and I wish you to agree with them. Understood?"

The Darlings nodded. The captain flung her nail file across the bridge. It stuck in the steering wheel, quivering. "All right," she said, "you asked for it. Are you sitting comfortably? Then I'll begin."

"Well," said the captain. "We are, as you have seen, a ship full of honest burglars, trying to scratch a living in this troublesome world. And it is not easy, let me tell you. Burglars with a vision—"

"Ahem," said Daisy sternly.

"Sorry," said the captain. "Where was I?"

"Burglars, not visions," said Daisy. "Stick to the point."

"Ah, yes. We have given up violence, mostly. But it is in our nature to nick stuff. We get into houses and have it away with the spoons and other valuables. Disguised as nannies." A curious look came into the captain's eye—a little sideways and almost shifty.

"Hardly sporting," said Daisy.

"Less of that," said the captain. "We nick from the rich and give to the poor, which is us. And reflect. Only rich families have nannies. And only families who are creepy as well as rich would ever ring up a nanny agency they have never heard of and get a complete stranger round to look after their children while they go out to dinner."

"Or to Antigua," said Daisy grimly.

"Or, as you say, to Antigua. But there is a problem." The captain sighed. "In life one finds so many. My burglars are a trusting bunch of lads and lasses, kind to small children and animals. Most of them are all right at self-defense, and I flatter myself that we have among our number some pretty capable muggers. But they simply cannot believe the stupidity and cruelty of nannies or the vicious cunning of children who have been brought up by them. They were shocked by your lecture, Daisy."

"They needed to be," said Daisy.

"Wet behind the ears," said Primrose.

"Like babes unborn," said Cassian.

"It is better to be a naive nanny than no nanny at all," said the captain. "My burglars bring an evening of sweetness and light to children while robbing their parents. Is that so very wrong?"

"Yes, it is," said Daisy. "Because nannies without proper training are going to get hurt. Leaving this aside for the moment, what is all this stuff about teddy bears?"

A curious rigidity spread over the captain's skillfully made-up features. "Bears?" she said.

"One particular bear," said Daisy. "Known, unless I am greatly mistaken, as the Royal Edward."

"Royal Edward?"

"Whose bum was stolen by Nanny Pete from our nursery. And whose left leg Nanny Huggins removed from the di Costaplenti residence this very day."

"Ah," said the captain, and looked deeply shifty. "Yes. That Royal Edward. Quite a prize."

"In what way?"

"A classic. A great classic. The finest-ever product of the legendary Bavarian bearsmith Gustav Barbauer, with plush head, agate eyes, and a voice box modeled on the larynx of the great Russian bass Chaliapin. Barbauer was bearsmith by appointment to the crowned heads of Europe during the golden age of bears, which is to say the early twentieth century, before the arrival of upstarts like Teddy Ruxpin and Pooh. Russian archdukes fled into exile clutching their Gustavs. Queen Victoria was never without hers till the day she died. Edward VIII's only quarrel with Mrs. Simpson was nothing to do with his abdication of the crown of England. It was about who got to kiss his Gustav and push its tummy so it said, '*Gute Nacht*, Your Royal Highness.' The only Gustav ever to come on the open market, known as the Royal Edward, arrived by dubious means after the abolition of the

Icelandic monarchy. A revolutionary plot, by all accounts; the bear was stolen, sold for three shiploads of dried cod to an unscrupulous middleman, and turned up at a LORP tombola in Happy Valley—"

"Meaning what?" said Daisy.

"I beg your pardon? Oh. LORP is a self-help organization founded to help people come to terms with massive personal wealth. It stands for the League of Rich People. A tombola is a sort of lottery."

"But why is the bear in bits?"

The captain gave the Darlings a sad, beautiful smile. "Because rich people are bad losers. There was a frightful battle when the winner was announced. When the dust settled, the Royal Edward had been torn into seven pieces and the people with the bits had jumped out of the windows and sprinted into the night, or anyway as far as their limousines."

"How extraordinarily silly," said Daisy.

"Quite so," said the captain. "But the only person sillier than the last rich person you met is the next rich person you meet, I always find. Anyway, I regard this as a great tragedy. And I have made it my mission in life to pinch back the bear bits and return them to their rightful owner."

"This Iceland bloke."

"His Serene and Royal Highness the Crown Prince Beowulf of Iceland, Holder of the Order of the Codfish and Volcano First Class, M.Sc. (Marine Engineering), Reykjavík."

"I see," said all three children, though frankly, they did not. "Easy as that, then. Nothing in it for you."

"Well," said the captain.

"Well what?"

"This is indeed the most valuable bear in the world. Smoothby's the auctioneers would give their eyeteeth to get hold of it. Possessing all its pieces would have its . . . rewards."

"Ah," said Daisy. "And are you the only person trying to get hold of it?"

There was an embarrassed silence. "Not exactly," said the captain finally.

"Hence the white van," said Daisy.

It worked a treat. The captain's mouth fell open. "What do you know about the white van?" she said.

"What you are going to tell us."

The captain shook her head wearily. "All right," she said. "I can see you're not the sort of people one can hide things from. The fact of the matter is, they want the Edward too."

"But who are they?"

"White Van Dan," said the captain. "And Hilda the Builder. And the Firm."

"Who?"

"It started a year ago. We were happy then. We'd just started AAA Aardvark. The boys and girls loved the dressing up, and we were just knocking off knickknacks, you know.

Then all of a sudden we heard that after we had, ahem, finished at a premises, someone would come along and tear out a side wall and move in with heavy equipment and not so much knock off knickknacks as knacker the gaff. Not a brick left standing on brick," said the captain. "Apparently they used to go round doing building work and pinching the silver. Then they started to flatten the houses with some huge machines they built, and pick the swag out of the rubble, and get the contract to rebuild the houses, and very badly they do it too, because all their machinery's breaking down, and they don't know how to mend it so it works. Then just at the wrong moment they heard about the Edward and they started following us around, getting bits of it. Any minute now, people will be blaming us for their burglaries."

Primrose said, "You mean they knock down the house to get at the stuff inside?"

"Go and have a look at what's left of One, Avenue Marshal Posh."

"No, thank you," said Cassian. "We much prefer it here."

"Dear child," said the captain. "Have a cigar. No? Ah, well. So anyway, our name is mud."

"And what about the police?" said Daisy.

"Who?"

"The filth," said Cassian.

"The fuzz, the cuffies, the Old Bill," said Primrose. "The long arm of the law, the busies. The boys in blue."

"Oh, I see," said the captain. "That lot couldn't find a boiled egg on a billiards table; do me a favor. But really, business is terrible—you wouldn't believe."

"Hmm," said Daisy. "Quite. How many bits of the Edward have they got?"

"One," said the captain. "The right arm."

"Well? You've got three, haven't you?"

"Couldn't you copy one?"

"No," said the captain. "It wouldn't smell right."

"Smell?"

"Experts are experts," said the captain, and assumed an expression of such distress that even Daisy could not bring herself to probe further.

"So you've got to get the arm back and steal the rest of the bear."

"Yes. Three more bits."

"And you know who's got them?"

"We do."

"And do the White Van Mob?"

"Not as far as I know. We think it works this way. Whenever the Jag goes out with the duty nanny, a builder spots them and passes the word—"

"Any builder?"

"They're all in it. Heard of the Freemasons? It's a sort of secret society. Masons, builders, same difference. So out comes the white van, extra-large size, a sort of mobile garage, really, with digger, dumper, and dozer. And down comes the house. They're usually too late, of course; did you ever hear of a builder arriving on time? And their van keeps breaking down. But that doesn't stop 'em trying."

"So how did they get the arm?" said Daisy.

"Nanny ex-navy. Charming chap, used to be a pirate. Got followed to a job by the white van. Pure coincidence. The builders pulled the arm from the ruins by sheer unscrupulous site work."

Daisy stood up. "Thank you, Captain," she said. "You have given us much to ponder."

"*Il n'y a pas de quoi,*" said the captain, with Old World courtesy. "Daisy, could we do some nanny tests to make sure the chaps are up to scratch? In about half an hour?"

"Willingly," said Daisy. The captain left.

There was a silence.

Naturally, it was Daisy who spoke first. "That was a load of cobblers," she said.

"Codswallop," said Primrose.

"Sheer 100 percent disinformation," said Cassian.

"Most of it, anyway," said Daisy. "We have here a Captain of Burglars who is stealing the parts of a royal bear in order to reassemble it for the delight of an ex–crowned head of Iceland. A pretty minor ex–crowned head, I may say, in no position to do her a favor. Well?"

"Tell it to the marines!" said Primrose.

"Pshaw!" said Cassian.

"And White Van Dan and the builders," said Daisy. "They may exist. But why would they want a bear?"

"Rubbish," said Primrose.

"Bizarrely hard to credit," said Cassian, scowling.

"And the bear's arm—"

"Which cannot be forged because of the wrong pong—"

"Bit strong!" said Cassian. "I mean, what does it matter what it smells like?"

"Quite. And finally," said Daisy, "how does she know about this LORP tombola? I mean, unless she was there?"

"And her a career burglar," said Primrose.

"Highly improbable," said Cassian. He frowned, as far as it was possible to tell. "And yet . . ."

"Yes?" said Daisy.

"Spit it out," said Primrose.

"I know it sounds silly. But, you know, I sort of . . . trust her."

Another silence, deeply shocked and rather embarrassed. Finally, Primrose said, "Know what you mean."

Daisy sniffed and pursed her lips. But she knew what Cassian meant, too. There was something about this captain.

"And another thing," said Cassian. "The chief engineer's got a bear's head in his control room."

More silence, devoted to the adjusting of ideas.

Finally Daisy stuck her chin in the air, expressing impatience. "Can't be doing with all this humbug and thinking and so on," she said. "We watch and wait and speak when spoken to and be a bit seen and not at all heard."

The other two nodded, soothed by this high-grade nanny talk.

"And when the time is ripe," said Daisy, "we pounce."

"What on?" said Primrose.

"Stop asking stupid questions," said Daisy. "Now. Time for the nanny test. Gather your equipment, and let's save some lives."

The tests were over by teatime. The captain came in. "You have done marvelously well," she said. "I am sure it must have been very taxing. Did any of them pass?"

"Two," said Daisy. "Plenty of doubtfuls and improvers. But only two certainties, which is to say Pete Fryer and Giant Luggage. Though Giant Luggage, well . . ."

"Quite," said the captain, raising her hands.

"The handle," said Daisy. "The size. The hat is not worn properly because of the handle. The size is large."

"Beautifully put," said the captain.

Daisy pursed her lips. "I always do say you should call a spade a spade," she said.

The captain frowned. "Daisy," she said, "a personal question. But . . . do you ever feel you might be *turning into* a nanny?"

"Heaven forbid!" cried Daisy.

"Yes," said Primrose. "We do. We can see it."

"How dare you!" cried Daisy. "You can both go to bed without your—"

"See?" said Cassian.

Daisy felt suddenly exhausted. She leaned against the captain, who smoothed her hair. "There, there," said the captain. "These are powerful forces, and we tamper with them at our peril."

At that moment there threaded among the late-afternoon sunbeams the silvery tinkle of the AAA Aardvark Nanny Line.

The captain made a gesture. Daisy glided swiftly to the bridge. Pete Fryer was there, receiver to ear. "Hold on a minute, ta, modom," he said, and handed the telephone to Daisy.

"Kin ai hep yew?" said Daisy.

The person on the other end was sneezing. "Sorry," said a man's voice. "Guitar string up my nose."

"How painful," said Daisy, with authentic nanny coldness. "Hau kin ai hep yew?"

"Nanny needed," said the voice. "'Ullo? Who am I talking to?"

"AAA Aardvark Child Minding and Security," said Daisy. "Just like you were before."

"Nice one," said the voice. "Listen, man, I can't find anyone. I was wondering if you could maybe get round here and, like, find someone?"

"Someone?"

"Like, the kids?"

"Are they lost?"

"Mislaid. Yeah, orright, lost."

"The address?"

"Stratocaster Hall, Oncebitten Golf Club."

"And the name?"

"Eric Thrashmettle. Prolly heard of me. Listen, I got to go out now. Key's under mat, right?"

"Thank you," said Daisy, making a note. "I shall just check."

"Thrashmettle?" hissed the captain, at her ear. "Eric? They were at the bear tombola. Get the job."

"Ai am happy to say," said Daisy, "that we will be there in fifteen minutes."

"Who's that?"

"Still AAA Aardvark."

"Oh. Yeah. Too much." The telephone went down.

There was the usual palaver. Bells rang, booted feet thundered on steel staircases, and the captain's voice on the loudspeaker said in a flat, metallic voice, "Duty nanny to the Jag deck." Actually, the levels of noise were unnecessary now that the duty nannies were down to two. But (as the captain pointed out) burglars love a bit of an emergency, or they would not have become burglars in the first place.

"What do you think?" said Daisy to her brother and sister as she charged up her stun gun in the suite.

"Weird," said Cassian.

"Something stinks," said Primrose.

"So we take a long, hard look," said Daisy. "And we report back."

"Later," said Primrose.

"Later."

"Later."

And there were Daisy and Nanny Pete, in the Jag, speeding toward Stratocaster Hall.

Cassian's heart got steadily lighter as the carpets ran out and the stairs turned to iron and he clomped ever deeper into the *Kleptomanic*'s innards; assuming, that is, that he had a heart. He himself was not sure. There was something in his chest that ticked away and seemed at bad times to be made of lead and at less bad times to be made of something lighter, aluminum maybe. Whether or not it was a heart, he could not say and did not, frankly, give a monkey's—

I beg your pardon. It is traditional to start new sections of a book in an arty fashion, setting the scene and giving the reader an idea of the mood of the person whose actions you are about to describe. The message here has got nothing to do with innards or ball bearings. The fact was that as Cassian got closer to the engine rooms, he felt happier, because engines were his favorite thing.

Clear?

Good.

On we go.

Giant Luggage was on the stokehold floor. He was dressed in nanny gear, now much stained with coal dust, and shoveling coal into a boiler. Cassian had just about worked out which boilers ran which engines. He had also crawled around the engines themselves, which seemed to him to be in an excellent state of maintenance and repair. Cassian hated to see a machine lie idle. He said to Giant Luggage, "Shall we turn her over?"

Giant Luggage said, "Hur, hur," which was just about all he ever said. There was a small scurry on the pile of coal, and Nosy Clanger appeared. "Can't be done," he said.

"But surely—"

"Fwitchgearf in the chief 'f control room," said Nosy. "E'f on ftrike."

"Pay?" said Cassian. "Conditions? What's his problem?"

"Unhappy man," said Nosy. "Ever finfe he loft hif—"

"Aieee!" cried a great voice from the control room. The door flew open. The chief engineer stood there, eyes rolling wildly. He was dressed in a uniform covered in gold braid, with a spiked helmet on his head. He was sucking his thumb.

"Fee?" said Nosy.

"Not to touch nuffink," shrieked the chief round his thumb. *"Nuffink."*

Cassian had a brief but powerful urge to smack the

chief's bottom and send him to his room to eat dry bread and water. Then he realized that that was a bit of leakage from Daisy. Besides, the chief was three times his size. So he decided to play the never-failing Interested Child card. "Gosh," he said. "What a super uniform. I am really interested in triple-expansion condensing steam engines. I have got a fantastic collection of Ships of the World bubble gum cards and my heart's desire is to see a ship like this actually working."

The chief took his thumb out of his mouth and allowed his mad brown eyes to rest on eager wee Cassian. "Insect," he said.

"No, really, actually," said Cassian. "If I am not mistaken, this is the kind with the modulating pitch valve, and—"

"Silence!" cried the chief loudly. "*Nobody touches the engines but me not even with their eyes and if you talk to me any more I will hold my breath till I am dead and then you will be sorry.*"

"Ah," said Cassian. This large person seemed to be malfunctioning in some way, but it was beyond his skill to work out how. If he had been a machine, it would have been different, of course. Well, perhaps Primrose could make one of her special mixtures to calm him down. Better still, Daisy could perhaps come and give him a good talking-to.

But Primrose was in the kitchens, doing research on the ideal pizza. And Daisy was far away, doing her nanny duty. . . .

Later, thought Cassian. Meanwhile, it would be just as well to familiarize himself with the machinery. There was probably some switchgear in the world that Cassian was unable to short-circuit, but he had not yet come across it. Research was what was needed. Research and preparation.

Cheered, he clambered up an iron ladder and disappeared into the belly of the machine.

The Jag hurtled through the night. Neither of its bowler-hatted occupants noticed a man high on a scaffolding drinking tea and swinging his feet. The man stuffed his copy of the *Daily Nudes* into the pocket of his overalls, climbed into a van, and accelerated after the Jag. As he drove, he unhooked a microphone. "Target in sight," he said.

Silence.

"I said, target in sight."

"Who are you calling a git?" said a furious voice.

"Target. As in black Jag."

"Why didn't you say so?" said the voice.

"I did."

"Dint."

"Did."

"Shut up and follow them," said the voice. "Note their destination. We'll send a backup team."

"Oh yeah, right," said the man in the van, continuing the pursuit. Builders always said they were going to turn up, but they hardly ever did. He would believe it when he saw it.

Stratocaster Hall seemed to be somewhere in the suburbs. The buildings were thinning out, the headlights freezing owls and rabbits in their white cones. Daisy, in the passenger seat, sniffed disapprovingly. "Nice carving," said Pete.

"I beg your pardon?"

"Carving knife, wildlife," said Pete Fryer, bowler brim low over the steering wheel.

"Wild animals are disorderly and wrong. A disgrace, in fact."

"I quite like them myself," said Nanny Pete.

"Suitable animals for children are tortoises and guinea pigs," said Daisy.

"Noted," said Nanny Pete, sneaking a glance at his young companion's resolute nanny profile.

"And by the way," said Daisy, introducing a question the captain had not chosen to touch on. "What's wrong with the chief engineer?"

"Chief?" said Nanny Pete. "Highly strung, like so many engineers. A man with a good heart, sorely wounded by life, haunted by a deep sense of personal betrayal."

"What *are* you talking about?" said Daisy, full of nanny impatience.

"He had a loss," said Pete. "Feels it deeply, very deeply indeed. He thinks the world has done him a great wrong—here we are!"

He stamped his nanny brogue on the brake. The Jag went into a tearing skid and shot between a pair of white marble pillars with statues on top. The lights glanced over a bronze plaque that said ONCEBITTEN PRIVATE ESTATE AND GOLF COURSE—THE RICH AND FAMOUS ONLY—NO HAWKERS, NO CIRCULARS, NO RUBBISH. A security guard bowed deeply. A long white road snaked through groves of astonishingly rare trees. Huge houses stood back from the road, buried in priceless shrubbery.

Behind the Jag, a small van shot through the gates, shouted, "Builders!" to the security guard, gave him two fingers, and began to crawl after the distant red eyes of the nannies' rear lights.

"Rock-and-roll heaven," said Nanny Pete. "Plus the odd dictator. The very odd dictator, actually. Bloke called Ponque. Reckons it's his job to conquer the world, using poultry instead of soldiers. Oi, oi. Wozzis, then?"

A curious figure had slouched out of a driveway ahead. It had very long hair and a face the color of lard. It was wearing a singlet, flared trousers, a belt with a huge Celtic buckle, snakeskin boots, and dark glasses. Having come out of the driveway, it turned sharp right, walked into a tree, and apologized. Then it marched out in front of the Jag.

Nanny Pete brogued the brakes. The Jag stopped, just touching the flares of the long-haired person's trousers. "Goodness," said Daisy. "It's Death Eric."

"Death who?" said Nanny Pete.

"Eric Thrashmettle," said Daisy. "Something of an idol of my brother, Cassian, though of course I think he is too silly for words." She rolled down the window. "Mr. Thrashmettle!" she cried in a stern nanny voice. "We have arrived to care for your children!"

"What children?" said Death Eric.

"Yours."

"Oh," said the rock-and-roll hero. "Yeah. I've lost 'em."

"We are terribly sorry to hear that."

"Yeah," said Death Eric. "We was, like, watching TV and when the program finished, I was, like, where the bleep are they? And I was, like, I dunno, do I? So I ring the agency."

"And here we are!" cried Daisy brightly. "So let us find your children, shall we, and put your mind at rest!"

"This way," said the long-haired man, walking into a rhododendron.

"Take off your dark glasses, why don't you?" said Daisy.

"Wha?"

"Lose the shades," said Nanny Pete.

"Oh." Death Eric took off his glasses and stood blinking in the light of the streetlamp. "Yeah."

"Now, then."

"Leave the wheels," said Death Eric. "C'mon." He led them down the drive and up to the front of a large, dark house. He turned the front door handle. "Locked out," he said.

"Where are your keys?"

"Dunno."

"Ahem," said Nanny Pete discreetly. "If I might be permitted?" He fumbled a moment with the lock. The door swung open. A burglar alarm began to shriek.

"Far out!" said Death Eric, tapping a snakeskin toe to the alarm's infectious rhythm.

Nanny Pete fumbled with the burglar alarm, which stopped. Death Eric nodded and grinned. "Okay," he said. "Find the kids, right? I'll be watching TV." He plonked himself down in a huge chair in the hall and groped for the remote. Yatter, yatter, yatter went the TV. Eric's jaw dropped. His eyes goggled. He became Elsewhere.

The nannies searched the house.

It was, in Daisy's view, an odd house for a rock star. There were a lot of military uniforms and photographs of guns and bombs. There were various golden trinkets and a few loose jewels, which Pete swept into his nanny case. But there seemed to be no nursery. And no children. And absolutely no limb of the Royal Edward. It was all (thought Daisy, tutting) most peculiar.

So downstairs they went. The TV was still blaring away in the hall, Death Eric slumped in the mighty lounger, his lips moving as he talked along with a *Teletubbies* repeat. Nanny Pete said, "Blowed if I understand."

"Me neither," said Daisy, with a callous disregard for grammar. "Is something wrong?"

For Nanny Pete was gazing at a picture on the wall.

It was a big picture, in a heavy gold frame. It was a picture of a man in military uniform crusted with gold. He was standing on a rock, saluting, an odd salute, right arm extended, three fingers in the air, halfway between the Nazis and the Scouts. In front of the rock was a large field. The field was full of chickens. They seemed to be listening to a speech the man was making.

"Poultry," said Nanny Pete pensively. There was a pause. Then he bellowed, "Mister Thrashmettle?"

"Yur," said Mr. Thrashmettle absently.

"Are you sure this is your house?"

"Wodjermean?" said Death Eric, not moving his eyes from the screen.

Briskly Daisy hauled the TV plug out of the wall.

"Oi!" cried Death Eric, gazing around him wildly. Then, "What are we doin' here?"

"You may well ask," said Daisy.

"In the house of Erminegildo Ponque, the Odd Dictator," said Nanny Pete. "And Mr. Thrashmettle lives—"

"I live next door!" said Death Eric. "Wodjew playin' at?"

They tumbled onto the front steps. "Over, like, here," he said, and began crashing through the shrubbery.

Daisy frowned. Behind the sound of splintering rhododendrons there seemed to be a distant grind of very big engines.

Death Eric patted his pockets. "No keys," he said.

"They're under the mat," said Daisy.

"Howdja know that?"

"You told me."

But Eric's soupy mind was already far away. He opened the front door and walked across the marble-floored hall and into a room with a bloodred shag-pile carpet and a conversation pit, in which conversation would not have been audible because of the TV, which was turned up all the way. "They was in here!" bellowed Death Eric.

"Who?"

"The kids."

"You mean the kids on the sofa over there?"

"Yeah." Death Eric's face broke into a muddy grin of relief.

Daisy found the remote and turned off the TV. Both the children turned round and started screaming at her to turn it back on. *"Silence!"* she cried.

Their little jaws dropped. Their little eyes widened. Nobody had ever talked to them like that before.

"Your poor papa lost you," said Daisy. Far above in the house, she could hear bumping noises. That would be Pete Fryer, searching for bits of Royal Edward.

"Course he did," said the elder of the two children, a fat little brute with cross-eyes and a button nose. "He forgot to look."

"Look where?"

"To his left."

"You were on the left?" said Death Eric. "You normally, like, sit on the right."

"Not this time," said the boy, who seemed to be the elder of the two children. "Silly old hippie." He began to play an imaginary Fender, sticking out his tongue.

"Heir guitar," said Death Eric, shaking his head wearily. "Comes of being brought up by roadies."

"Where's their mother, for goodness' sake?"

"California," said Death Eric. "Or maybe Rome. Who can tell?"

"Dearie me," said Daisy briskly. The noises upstairs were continuing. And there was another noise, a large, mechanical noise, from outside. "Well, children. Nanny will burn you some nice custard, and then it's off to bed with—"

The noise outside was so loud that she could not finish the sentence. And she did not get a chance to try again, because at that moment, the wall of the room bulged inward and collapsed and someone drove a bulldozer into the conversation pit. It sat there, roaring and twitching.

"Wow," said Death Eric.

"Dearie me!" said Daisy.

Nanny Pete's head appeared round the door. "Scarper!" he cried.

Suddenly the room was full of dust and rubble and noise.

And builders: dozens of builders.

Daisy grabbed a child in each hand and scarpered through the hole in the wall and into the night.

"This way!" cried Pete from the darkness ahead. The night was full of engines, it seemed. Daisy started to ask the first of sixty questions. But she did not have the breath, and besides, it took all her strength to keep hold of the sticky little hands in hers. They were trying to get away, but she hung on for dear life. "On!" cried Nanny Pete.

"Coming!" she cried, dragging her little charges through the roaring night.

"Aargh!" cried Death Eric, who seemed to be crashing around in the rhododendrons. There was the sound of a body hitting a tree, and his voice said, "Sorry, man." Behind them, there was a slipping roar and a huge sproingg! "Me guitar collection!" cried Eric. Whap went another tree trunk. "Sorry, man," said Eric.

Then something was gleaming faintly in the light of the streetlamps, and the air smelled of hot oil, and there was the Jag, waiting.

"In!" cried Pete.

They piled in. The Jag roared away. Something huge and white loomed in the headlights: something the size of an articulated lorry. Bigger than a lorry.

"Bleeding white van," said Pete.

It was indeed a white van. A huge white van, doors open, great ramps down, the bonnet open, two ladders propped against it. "It's broken down!" cried Daisy.

"More 'n likely," said Pete. "Now, then, Death, where to?"

"They knocked the house down," said Daisy, dazed.

"We got plenty more," said Death Eric.

"Masses," said his kids.

So the nannies dropped them off at their penthouse flat in the middle of town and returned to the *Kleptomanic*.

"Did you get it?" said Daisy, in the cargo net.

"Jewels," said Pete. "Nice little mandolin, cuff links, nose rings—"

"The right leg of the Royal Edward?"

There was a short but well-filled silence. "Not as such," said Nanny Pete.

"So the white van people have."

Pete sighed. "More than likely," he said.

"Not a disaster, though," said Daisy.

"That's what you think," said Pete.

After that, the silence went on and on. Finally, Daisy said, "What is it about the Royal Edward?"

"Valuable bear."

That old thing again.

Primrose was having a brilliantly experimental time in the kitchen. She had spent the afternoon with a kind lady called Sophie Nickit, working on a recipe for Sleepy Cake. Sophie was mixing away at a great bowl full of soothing blue mixture and chattering as she worked. "Yes, dear," she said, batting her queen-sized lashes. "I used to be a vamp and a roller."

"Papa and Secretary Mummy have got a Roller," said Primrose. "Do you think blue's the right color?"

"Bit bright," said Sophie. "Not that kind of roller. I used to meet chaps and pinch their wallets. Then I thought I'd run away to sea; I mean it's normally chaps do that, but why shouldn't us girls? Do you think pink would be better?"

"You bet," said Primrose. Sophie sighed, threw away the mixture, and started again, using powdered pink sleep moth instead of blue. "What do you mean, run away to sea?"

"This is a ship, you know."

Primrose nodded, stirring. Actually, she had just about forgotten. For her the *Kleptomanic* was kitchen heaven, full of extremely interesting people who let you follow up Lines of

Culinary Enquiry. "But why," she said, "have you not sailed away already?"

"Ask the chief engineer."

"Wha?"

"I mean, we're not ready yet." Sophie suddenly looked oddly confused.

"Ah," said Primrose, and changed the subject. When they tried the Sleepy Cake on the ship's hamster, the chubby rodent's wheel came to an immediate standstill, and it fell plunk to the cage floor.

But despite her enthusiasm for cookery, Primrose found it hard to keep her mind on the slumber of experimental animals. It was on other things, deeper and darker.

That evening, the little Darlings ate supper in the suite. It was another delicious repast, featuring lobster cocktail, toad-in-the-hole with tinned tomatoes, and five colors of yogurt with maple syrup. Normally, these excellent provisions would have inspired a merry buzz of conversation. Tonight, there was only a preoccupied silence.

"So," said Daisy. "They're trying to get all the bits of the bear, but they haven't."

"What I do not understand," said Primrose, "is why they haven't just started up the ship and sailed away somewhere interesting."

"Most disappointing," said Cassian. "She's in first-class mechanical order, of course."

"Which is more than can be said for the white van," said Daisy.

There was a silence.

Finally, Primrose said, "In the chief engineer's room. In that glass case with the eagle thing on top of it, that first time we went down there. What did it look like to you?"

"Bear's head," said Cassian.

"On a crimson velvet cushion," said Daisy.

"Yup."

A bit more silence. "Funny-looking chap, the chief engineer," said Daisy. "Distinctive."

The three of them summoned up a picture in their minds: a picture of a face with a nose ten centimeters long, a drooping lower lip, and wildly rotating chestnut-colored eyes under the peak of a blue-and-gold spiked hat.

"Tell you what," said Cassian. "Let's go and have a look at a couple of things in the ship's library."

"But it is way past our bedtime," said Daisy.

"Daisy!"

Off to the library they went.

They sat round a leather-topped table, coughing in the clouds of dust that rose from the volumes of *Burke's Steerage,* the famous reference book of the world's fallen aristocracy. They leafed. They stopped leafing and read. Daisy made a note. Then out of the library they trooped, onto the grand staircase.

"To the bridge," said Cassian.

"Hist!" said Daisy, raising a finger.

Through the quiet spaces of the ship there flowed a stream of music. The Darlings followed that stream to its source. They found themselves in the shadows on the fringes of the ballroom. A single spotlight shone on the grand piano on the stage. At the piano sat the captain in her red dress, transported.

The music wound to its end. The Darling children stepped forward as one child.

"Why!" said the captain, with a brilliant smile. "You were listening. How sweet!"

"Not sweet," said Daisy, over whom a nanny-like hardness had once again swept. "Not listening. Waiting."

"Ah," said the captain, closing the piano lid. "What for?"

"Here," said Daisy. Cassian pushed a chair to the piano. Daisy climbed onto it. Primrose handed her the volume of the *Encyclopaedia Kleptomanica* they had brought from the library. Daisy flopped the book open. Dust rose. "And what does this say?" said the captain, putting a long red fingernail on the place on the page where it said *For Reference Only— Not to Be Removed*.

"Nicked it, dint we," said Primrose.

"Well *done*," said the captain, beaming.

"Look at this," said Cassian.

They all looked, in the earnest way people do look when they know what they are going to see because they have seen it already.

There was a picture of a man and a woman. Both of them were wearing crowns and sitting on thrones made of some kind of dark rock, possibly volcanic. They wore the ribbons of Orders, on which were pinned silver reproductions of large fish. In the background, a volcano seemed to be erupting. The faces were long and blobby. The noses were ten centimeters long. The eyes, which were chestnut colored, were looking in four different directions, as if the photographer had caught them in mid-whirl.

"Remind you of anyone?" said Cassian.

"Weeell . . ." said the captain.

"Clue," said Daisy. "Somewhere under your feet."

"Sulking," said Primrose. "Sulking a lot."

"Er . . ." said the captain, putting a red nail on her red lower lip.

"Spell it out, Daisy," said Primrose.

"Your chief engineer," said Daisy, "is Crown Prince Beowulf of Iceland. And he is in a terrible sulk because someone has taken away his teddy."

"And part of this sulk is that he will not start the engines on this ship until someone gives him his teddy back."

"Which I would be well happy to do, having sewed it together with my busy needle," said Primrose. "Except that it strikes me that you do not have all the bits; am I right or am I right?"

The captain gazed upon them fondly, drawing a great rippling arpeggio from the keys. "Darlings, you are *so* right," she said. "And I am *so* proud of you!"

Normally, this kind of talk would have turned the thoughts of the little Darlings toward violence of a subtle but extreme type. But this time, they felt unaccountably happy. They sat smiling like idiots, waiting for the explanation.

"Well," said the captain, getting up. "Way past my bedtime, I think."

"Er . . ." said Cassian.

"But . . ." said Primrose

Daisy pursed her lips. "You will sit here until you have quite finished telling us everything there is to know!" she cried.

The captain blinked. Her eyes went glassy. "Yes, Nanny," she said. She frowned. "Goodness. Where am I?"

"Here," said Cassian.

"Now," said Primrose.

"Telling us what you know about the chief engineer," said Daisy. "Like a good girl, who was brought up by a Nanny Who Knew Best."

"How did you know?" sighed the captain.

"One presses the button," said Daisy. "One watches the victim light up."

"So shoot," said Primrose.

The captain shot.

"All right," she said. "But it's not a happy story."

"Happiness?" said Daisy. "What would that be?"

"Poor little Darlings," said the captain, and began.

10

"The revolution," she said. "A terrible thing, which I shall not begin to describe. Suffice it to say that Crown Prince Beowulf of Iceland escaped an outbreak of civil unrest by running away on a trawler bound for Aberdeen. But when going through his luggage at bedtime after his first dogwatch, he found that his treasured Gustav, the Royal Edward, was missing. Imagine," said the captain, "the horror of this poor, deprived person. His kingdom gone. His icy, fishy, volcanic heritage snatched away from him. And now his bear Edward—for at the end of it all, Gustavs are only bears, royal or not—snatched away. The bear he had sniffed and dribbled on ever since he had been a tiny baby—"

"Revolting," said Daisy.

"Sad," said Primrose.

"But entirely probable," said Cassian.

"Snatched away from him by the hand of an unrelenting nanny."

"A nanny?"

"It was the royal nanny who stole it. Seeing, one presumes, her pension going up in smoke as the mob ransacked the palace. Actually," said the captain, "I think that the Iceland situation was what gave me the idea of starting a nicking nanny crew. But that is another story. Any road," she said. "The Royal Edward came up as a prize at the LORP's tombola, as you know. Actually, I was there."

"How was that?" said Cassian, frowning.

"Very nice evening, if you like rich people."

"He means, how did you come to be there?" said Primrose.

"Someone drove me," said the captain.

"Excuse me," said Daisy, "but could you give a straight answer to a straight question?"

"No," said the captain. "Anyway. The Edward had been sold to a rich family by the ex-nanny of the royal family of Iceland. The rich family had got bored with it, had a moment of fashionable repentance—"

"What's that?" said Primrose.

"It's like going on a diet or going to a charity ball to help the homeless, all that," said Daisy. "Then you feel all right about making a pig of yourself or buying a lot of houses you don't need. Papa and Secretary Mummy do it all the time."

"They say it's like being reborn," said the captain. "So anyway, there was this sort of raffle, and all these rich people loved the Edward, and of course I recognized it instantly—only one of its kind in the world. Then there was a riot, and seven people started to fight over it. I sort of got the head while nobody was looking."

"But what were you doing at this tombola?"

"Playing the piano," said the captain. "Looking for suitable burglary victims. Anyway, a bit later I found this ship. I tracked the Crown Prince down, because he's an utterly brilliant engineer, thinking he'd be happy to have at least part of his bear; one does so like to spread a little happiness, you know. So I gave him the head. But it didn't work. Quite the opposite, actually. Every time he looked at it, it made him sad and mad and reminded him of the horror of his exile. So he's decided he won't start the engines until he gets the rest of it back."

"All of it?"

"All of it."

"And how much of it have we got?"

"Some of it."

"But we are missing . . ."

"The arms. The right leg. The torso."

"Where were they?"

The captain smiled, the sort of smile a monkey might give

you if you stood on its foot. "There are," she said, "certain bits in the possession of—"

"White Van Dan," said three voices at once—belonging (in reverse order of height) to Primrose, Daisy, and Cassian.

"And," said the captain, "I expect you would like to know about White Van Dan, too?"

The Darlings smiled at her sweetly. "We are sitting comfortably. Do please begin, Captain dear."

"Oi," said a voice in the shadows. "No way."

"Pete," said the captain, and it was indeed none other than Nanny Pete Fryer, wearing nanny uniform and a deep scowl of loyalty. "It is all right. These are clever children, and I must tell them what I know."

"If you must, you must," said Pete.

"Well," said the captain. "Let me take you back to the tombola that saw the division of the Edward. It was a large room, gracious, with a mighty chandelier, in a house on Avenue Marshal Posh. The myriad flames of the chandelier made rainbows in the jewelry of the assembled plutocrats. There was Bulgari, Yves Saint Laurent, Balenciaga, lashings of Versace; yes, Cassian, I shall get on with it if you stop yawning. And above it all, through a hole in the ceiling, there glittered a single eye. A bloodshot eye, children, an eye made sore by brick dust and smoke. The eye, in fact, of the bodger known as White Van Dan, who was patching a roof leak with a copy of the *Girls of the World,* which would stop the water as long as it did not rain, but what did he care?"

"Not a fig," said Primrose.

"Exactly," said the captain. "He watched the women with their jewels and the men with their diamond Rolexes. He meant to nick them all. He was not interested in the tombola. As far as he was concerned, the bear was a dusty old freak. He built his machines and started flattening houses to get at jewels. It was only later, when the machines began to break down, that the Edward became his life's obsession."

"Why?" said Cassian.

"For no very good reason, you may be sure," said the captain. "For a bad one, indeed, and to understand it, you have to know where White Van Dan comes from.

"They trace their ancestry to a certain Cesare Bodger, in Renaissance Italy. Cesare built many villas and churches. They all fell down, but Cesare did not care, because he made sure he got the ducats before the collapse. Generation followed generation, but the family traditions did not change. Until the present generation, when the evil genius White Van Dan discovered that instead of actually having to go somewhere and build something before he and his firm got their money, it was just as easy—nay, easier—to attack the houses of his clients with a digger, a dozer, and a dumper and scratch the loot out of the rubble, then secure the rebuilding contract." The captain shuddered delicately. "A coarse approach, without finesse," she said, and paused, gazing at scenes that by the look of her face were far away and painful.

"I do not understand," said Daisy, "why such awful villains would be troubling themselves with a teddy bear."

"Bodger by name, bodger by nature," said the captain. "White Van Dan and Hilda, his mate, designed and built a hugely sophisticated gaff-destroying tool, known as the White Van. At least, they think it's sophisticated. And it is, if your idea of nicking is to flatten gaffs and batter the loot. They are very, very stupid people."

"There is no excuse for stupidity," said Daisy.

"Except lack of brains," added Cassian.

"Quite. Anyway, they made this machine out of low-quality materials and old coat hangers, so it breaks down. They need an engineer of genius to maintain it and to help build a better one. The only great engineer they know of is our own Beowulf, ex–Crown Prince of Iceland. So they approached him with great blandishments, because they saw in him a chance not only to get their machines mended, but to gain effective control of a North Atlantic island surrounded by luxury-grade cod and studded with excellent volcanoes. They promised him that they would help restore him to the throne of Iceland and that they would build him a palace there. And most importantly, that they would restore to him the missing parts of the Royal Edward. Naturally, they had forgotten who had taken the parts home after the tombola brawl. So they took to following us around in the hope that we would lead them to bear parts." The captain looked grim. "With, I am sorry to say, some success."

"But you have nearly half the parts. The bum, the left leg, the head—"

"It is the chief who has the head. He claims that it is now the property of the kingdom of Iceland. Whoever restores unto him the other parts of the bear secures his services. Frankly, I think he longs to get his hands on all that rotten site machinery. He is a real enthusiast."

"Bravo!" murmured Cassian.

"Fie!" cried Daisy, her hand on her heart. "So we have only two bear bits out of a possible six. And whoever gets the parts and reassembles the Edward gets the chief?"

"Exactly so."

"And whoever loses—"

"Never say it!" cried the captain. "On the one hand, our kind and resourceful burglars. On the other, a bunch of builders who hate children and will fail to turn up to build a new loo for their granny if she is stupid enough to pay them in advance. The old, old battle, good against evil."

"I say," said Cassian. "How awfully sporting. Why," he said, a little later, "are you all glaring at me like that?"

"We just are," said the captain, Primrose, and Daisy.

"So what," said Cassian, somewhat red about the ears, "are you going to do about it?"

"Good question," said the captain. "There is an answer. But first, we must complete the collection of the bear bits."

"How many to go?"

"We must assume that we lost one tonight. To recap: we have the bum and the left leg."

"And they have an arm and a leg."

"Correct."

"Goodness me," said Daisy, whose head was spinning in a slow, whirling manner. "And what if we wind up even Steven, three each, and neither side wishes to concede?"

"According to the Statutes of Larceny, the side with the majority of bits has the opportunity to buy the other side's bits for the other side's nominee's weight in loot."

"And if you have equal numbers?"

"There will be a Challenge."

"Well, then."

"But that will not be necessary."

"How not?"

"Because I know where another arm is."

"Where?"

"In the house of Cosmo Stuff, Minister for People."

"Wow," said Cassian. "A politician."

"Exactly so."

"Our papa knows him," said Cassian. "I have seen his cars. Nasty pieces of American junk they are, too."

"Cassian!" said Daisy. "No emotions here, if you please."

"Frightfully sorry."

"But the thing is," said the captain, "we can't just sit around and wait for the Stuffs to ring up, because it might never happen. Of course they're on the nanny blacklist. But the nanny they've got at the moment has done seven years in the Special Air Service What she doesn't know about violence and sarcasm is not worth knowing, and she will be hard to shift."

"One is always anxious to persuade such authorities to pass their knowledge on," said Daisy, simpering horribly.

"And a nanny is often partial to a cup of tea and a home-made bun," said Primrose. "What eh, Daise?"

"Nice one, Primrose," said Daisy. "Off you go to your kitchens!"

"What is going on?" said the captain.

"Wait and see," said Daisy.

The captain smiled. "Really, darlings," she said, "you are so reassuring!"

There was a man with a pickax in a trench, hacking away. He neither knew nor cared what the trench was for. All he knew was that he had been digging it for a week, and that it was a short trench, and that he had nearly gone down into the ground as far as the tops of his boots. The man took two more swipes, then leaned on his pick, looking down the street of large suburban houses peeping whitely from among their swimming pools and shrubberies. As he watched, a black Jag hurtled past him, jammed on the anchors, and came to rest outside the gates of a house that looked as if someone had grafted bits of Ancient Rome onto bits of Merrie England.

The man in the trench pulled out a phone and dialed. "Dick the Pick," he said. "Alert. Alert." Braced by this exciting event, he spat on his hands, hefted the pick, and took a giant swipe at a cylindrical object running across the trench. There was a hiss and a roar, and a white jet shot thirty meters into the air. "Water main," said Dick the Pick somewhere in his slow head. "Nice one." He sat down, took a thermos out of his bag, and poured himself a cup of tea. He felt he deserved it.

Daisy closed the Jag door, straightened her bowler, and took the pram out of the boot. There was a bit of a racket coming from down the road, where a small car seemed to be dancing on a large fountain that had suddenly come into being alongside a striped builder's tent. But Daisy in nanny mode had more important things than fountains on her mind. As Nanny Pete drove the Jag away, she began to push the pram slowly down the pavement.

It was three o'clock in the afternoon, an hour at which (Daisy calculated) children would have finished their Afternoon Sleeps whether they liked it or not and would be on the point of being dragged out for a Nice Walk Before

Tea. Sure enough, she had not gone far with her pram when she heard the crunch of brogues on gravel and the whimper of tiny voices. She slowed the beat of her own brogues and leaned forward, adjusting the pink balaclava that concealed the face of the doll in the pram.

"Mush!" said a powerful, grating voice behind her. "Git along, ye hounds of hell!" Fixing a sweet smile to her face, Daisy looked over her shoulder. And there were a little girl and a little boy wearing overcoats in regulation pink and blue, with little velvet collars and little white socks. On top of the overcoats were harnesses decorated with sweet bunnies. Holding the reins of the harnesses was a large and terrifying nanny, with a bowler hat pulled far down over her ears, hollow cheeks, and a hatchet nose.

"Afternoon, Nanny!" said Nanny Daisy.

"Afternoon, Nanny!" said the nanny with the nose. Then, to the children, "Giddap, ye miserable sinners."

"Noooo!" wailed the little children.

"Sprigs of damnation," said the nanny. "Didn't finish up their nice lunches. Very, very wrong. Their poor mummy and daddy. Work their fingers to the—"

"Tch, tch," said Daisy, wagging her own bowler. "Ingratitude is a shameful thing. So that's you in there, is it?"

"With Sir Cosmo and Lady Stuff," said the nanny, who seemed to be slightly Scots. "Ai am Nanny Pierrepoint. And you?"

Daisy simpered. "I hope through diligent niceness and cruelty to work my way up to your dizzy heights. Nowadays we are at Mrs. Cringe's."

"Ai don't think we know Mrs. Cringe."

"Not entirely suitable," said Daisy, sniffing. "But we have hopes."

Nanny Pierrepoint gave her a nod in which superiority was mixed with respect for the decent ambitions of the younger generation. "Never give an inch," she said.

"Just what I always say," said Daisy. "Thank you for your excellent advice!"

"Hoot, toot," said Nanny Pierrepoint. "We must all start somewhere, I think."

"Nanny!" said the little girl. "I need to—"

"Speak when you're spoken to!" snarled Nanny Pierrepoint.

Daisy decided that she had had about all she could stand of this villainous battle-ax. "Shall we sit down?" she said. "You could give me some tips. And I have a tiny little basket of tea and cakes."

"The children do not eat between meals," said Nanny Pierrepoint.

"Who said anything about children?" said Nanny Daisy.

Nanny Pierrepoint's hand smote her a mighty blow between the shoulder blades. "That's my gal!" she cried. "Whoa there, reptiles! Let's sit on this bench!"

They sat. Nanny tethered her charges to a bench leg. Daisy hauled from under the pram a basket covered with a cloth embroidered with fuchsias, larkspur, and (she saw, to her horror) a skull and crossbones. "Sweet cloth," said Nanny Pierrepoint. "Fuchsias, larkspur, and—"

"Tulip bulbs," said Daisy, hiding the cloth quickly—really, burglars were hard to trust, even with embroidery needles. "One lump or two?"

"One," said Nanny, accepting the delicate china cup.

"Cake?" said Daisy, offering a tin of Primrose's Sleepy Fairy Cakes with pink icing.

"Ooh," said Nanny Pierrepoint, slavering. "Don't mind if Ai do." She took a cake and ate it with the ends of her teeth, like a vast, bony squirrel. It vanished in no time.

"Another?" said Daisy.

"Och, I shouldn't really," said Nanny Pierrepoint, simpering horribly and taking two.

"Us," whimpered the little boy, stirring at the end of his leash.

"Not suitable," snapped Nanny Pierrepoint.

Daisy held her breath. Primrose had been quite definite. One cake for a doze. Two for a sound sleep. Three for a two-week holiday in dreamland . . .

Nanny Pierrepoint's eyes rolled up in her head, and she crashed to the ground like a nasty old tree. Daisy searched her, found her keys, and rolled her into the bushes. Then she untied the poor little children, put the lid on the Sleepy Cake tin, and opened another, full of Primrose's best Archangel Cakes, acknowledged by all lucky enough to consume one as the most delicious things in heaven or on earth. "Well," said Daisy. "I'm Nanny Daisy, darlings. So dig in and then we'll go home."

"Hooray for Nanny Daisy!" cried the tinies, punching their little fists in the air. They scarfed the cakes with amazing swiftness. "Thank you, Nana," they said, the joy of snacks shining from their poor little eyes.

"Now, then," said Daisy. "Off we go, and you can watch TV if you like."

"We're not allowed," said the little boy sadly.

"You are today," said Daisy. She found she was beaming. It was not something she had done for ages, and it did not hurt her face as much as she had thought it would.

But there was serious stuff on hand, so she unbeamed and fixed a small, smug nanny smile on her face. She followed the footprints in the gravel round the side of the house and opened the door marked NURSERY. She shooed the children in, went after them into a small hall full of the smell of boiled cabbage, and headed toward the uncarpeted stairs that wound upward, presumably toward the nursery floors. She hoped they had a TV in the nursery. People had broken enough promises to the little Darlings to make her very keen on keeping any she made.

A door swung open. Brilliant light streamed into the dingy hall. "Nanny!" cried a huge, fruity voice. "Come and bring the children with you, if you would be so kind, damn you!"

The speaker was a man, with a shiny white smile and a shiny dark suit. His eyes were warm and twinkling, and it seemed to Daisy that he had known her for years. Then she realized that what he was seeing was not Daisy but a nanny, any old nanny, or possibly a voter, any old voter.

"Children!" she trilled. "Daddy wants you!"

The children went into the hall, mumbling sullenly. They were too young to vote and therefore expected no mercy. "Here we are!" cried the daddy. "My little ones! Torquil and Nevada!"

"Utah!" cried the little girl.

"Ha, ha!" laughed the daddy, catching the little ones by the hands and spinning them to face a man with a TV camera. "Yes, I am passionately attached to my children. I think it is so important. Education begins at home. Speak to me in Latin, Torquil!"

"No," said Torquil, sticking out a lower lip like a church doorstep.

"Brilliant!" cried the daddy.

"And where is Lady Stuff?" said the man beside the camera.

"Shopping," said the daddy. "Enjoying the fruits of my party's splendid economic revolution!"

Utah burst into tears. *"I want my mummy,"* she howled. *"She went off with the man who teaches her horse riding and she said she is never coming back. I want my—"*

"Ha, ha!" chortled the daddy heartily. "Kids, eh?" Then, in a lower voice, "Lose 'em."

"Where's their TV?" said Daisy in a low hiss. "And the left arm of the Royal Edward? They'd like to play with it."

The political smile turned grim and stretched. "Do your job," he said.

"I'll argue."

"You're sacked."

"Later I'm sacked." Daisy drew breath, turned to the camera, and opened her mouth.

"Noooo," said the daddy. "In there." He pointed to a door. There was the noise of engines in the drive. The smile flicked back onto his face, and he turned to the camera. "And here come a few neighbors to tell me how much they love me and how they admire what I am doing for this great country of ours. A happy country is made of happy homes!"

Daisy shepherded the children through the door. There was an enormous TV and a huge buttoned-leather sofa. She turned on the TV.

"What's that?" said Torquil.

"Cartoons, dear."

"What's cartoons?" said Utah.

"That is."

The children nodded, attempting to grasp this brand-new idea. Daisy found them some chocolates, poured them Cokes from the drinks tray, and looked about her. Her heart beat once, hard, under her apron. High on the wine-red wall was a polished shield. On the shield was the left arm of the Royal Edward.

Marvelous.

Outside the window the roaring of engines had grown louder. The neighbors, no doubt, popping round to admire Sir Cosmo Stuff's teeth and achievements.

The sound became a noise. It got louder. It turned into an earsplitting roar. Daisy peeped out of the door just in time to see a bulldozer come through the closed front door and grind to a halt in the hall.

"Aiee!" cried Sir Cosmo, turning white with terror. He tried to run away, but he fainted first.

The cameraman kept right on filming.

Daisy shinnied up a set of bookcases and seized the shield with the arm. The tinies were clutching each other like the Babes on the Sofa. Normally, Daisy would have ignored the little brutes. But since being kidnapped by burglars, she had come to realize that kindness was a Good Thing, within reason. So she said, "Who looks after you when Nanny Pierrepoint has been drinking gin?"

"Nelly."

"Where's Nelly?"

"In her room. Knitting stuff. Will you take us there? We're frightened."

Daisy scowled at the infants. There was a perfectly good window in this room, looking out on a nice dark shrubbery into which it would be easy to disappear. But even as she imagined disappearing, a face rose before her eyes: the face of the captain, brimming over with kindness. Stop it now, Daisy told herself. Be hard, be definite—but she found that there was a little hand in each of her hands. "Come on," she heard herself saying. "We'll find Nelly, then." And leaving the arm propped on the sofa, she dragged the little people across a hall full of noise and dust into the smelly back regions of the house, where they collided with a nice-looking girl with pink cheeks.

"Nelly!" shrieked the munchkins. Nelly folded them in a sickening hug. Elsewhere in the house, a wall crumbled with a roar.

"Bye!" cried Daisy, and rushed back into the hall. It seemed to be raining chandeliers. Thank you, nanny hat, she thought as a blizzard of crystals rattled on her head. The bulldozer was halfway up the stairs. The cameraman was looking at the place where his camera had been and no longer was. *Nicked*, thought Daisy. The wall of the TV room seemed to have vanished. She ran through it to pick up the arm from the sofa. . . .

The arm had gone.

She stood there with her mouth open.

She knew what had happened.

While she had been softly handing saucepan lids over to loving Nelly, the arm of the Royal Edward had fallen into the hands of White Van Dan.

Well, she would take it back.

Settling her bowler hat firmly on her head, she started back toward the dozer.

That was when the digger bucket came through the wall.

It was a miracle, really.

The bucket swiped the sofa. The sofa swiped Daisy. As if biffed by a huge leather boxing glove, she sailed out of the window. She hit the ground, rolled, and was on her feet immediately. When she looked at the house, she saw clouds of dust and gaping holes. As she watched, the hall collapsed on itself with a roar.

There was no sense going back in there. She had failed. Wearily, Daisy began to trudge back toward the Jag, which was rolling down the street toward her.

She was miserable.

The White Van Mob now possessed more of the Royal Edward than the nanny burglars, and there was only the torso to go. Daisy caught herself shuddering to think how disappointed everyone would be. It was a most unusual sensation.

And now she came to think of it, there was another thing. She had failed in her errand because she had shown kindness and concern for little Torquil and Utah.

What was happening to her?

It was a nervous, worried Daisy who loaded the pram into the Jag boot, heaved herself into the passenger seat, emptied her pockets of loose jewels and gold cigarette lighters, and allowed herself to be driven home.

"Looka dat," said Nanny Pete as they headed back down the road. Daisy could tell she was being cheered up, but she looked anyway.

A figure was crashing around in the bushes by the bench at the end of the road. Branches broke, and birds flew out. From the wreckage emerged a wide, flat person in a green uniform with starched white collar and cuffs, a heavily stained white apron, and a brown bowler hat. It was Nanny Pierrepoint.

Daisy watched, awestruck, as the nanny zigzagged out into the road. Three of the Sleepy Cakes should have left her in the Land of Nod for many a rosy day, but here she was, up and about, almost as good as new—(Nanny Pierrepoint fell over)—except for a slight dizziness.

Now she was up again, dusting herself down, scowling

around her, looking for little Stuffs to torment. But all she could see was a mushroom cloud of dust rising over the Stuff residence. She stood and gazed fuzzily at it, her bulldog jaw meeting her hatchet nose, the glint of stupidity dim in her eye as she tried to work out what the blue blazes was going on.

"Minim," said Nanny Pete in a quiet, thinking-aloud sort of voice.

"I beg your pardon?"

"Minim and crotchet, watch it," said Pete absently.

A dim shape had formed in the dust cloud: the shape of a huge white van. The clash of gears reached them and a dull booming, like a heavy gun or a huge engine backfiring. The boom became a roar. The dim shape became distinct. And down the road trundled the white van.

It trailed white smoke. Daisy knew, even without Cassian's help, that this meant its piston rings were shot to hell. At least two of its eighteen tires seemed to be flat, and its huge bonnet was flecked with rust, as if it had iron measles. Twin fluffy dice bounced in its windscreen. It was a shocking sight.

Certainly Nanny Pierrepoint seemed to think so. She stood in the middle of the road, scowling, as if preparing to ask why in the name of all that was cuddly this vehicle had on it neither pink bunny rabbits nor pale blue elephants. When it was nearly on her, she raised a raw-knuckled hand to stop it. The hand was still up as the white van smote her with its radiator, knocked her flat, and steamed away into the afternoon.

"Dearie me!" cried Daisy, for good children and nannies never swear.

"She's all right," said Nanny Pete. "Huge ground clearance, that white van. Didn't crunch her bones nor grind her limbs. Look, she's up!"

And indeed, Nanny Pierrepoint was sitting up. Her bowler hat was jammed down to her chin, and she was shaking her fist at a blackbird, which she had apparently mistaken for the white van. She was drenched in black sump oil from the white van's many leaks. *"Ai resign!"* she cried. She got up, reeled into a thicket of rhododendrons, and was seen no more.

"Home, James," said Nanny Pete to himself. The Jag shrieked away from the curb and shot down the road, fishtailing wildly. Half an hour later, Daisy was climbing out of the cargo net onto the launchpad.

"Any luck?" said the captain, svelte in dark green satin that matched her eyes, holding a shaker of emerald-colored liquid.

"Quite the reverse," said Daisy. "They got the left arm. I blame myself."

"Never do that," said the captain.

"It is a great pity," said Daisy, "and if you permit me, I shall do what I can to put it right."

"But of course," said the captain. "Cocktail? No? Well, you know best, I expect." And she disappeared into the ship.

Later, the Darlings heard the piano in the ballroom. "'Stormy Monday Blues,'" said Daisy.

"Sounds like she's got the blues, all right," said Primrose.

"Startling tragic intensity," said Cassian.

And Daisy knew that things were not going well, not at all.

Cassian was really getting to know the engine room. The machinery, from coal lump to safety valve, with a comprehensive list of the intervening bunkers, furnaces, tubes, pistons, con rods, valves, and condensers, sat in his head in all its steel and brass and perfect logic. He really thought he could have got steam up and started the engine without trying, except that only the chief engineer had control of the starting switch, and without the switch, there was just no way.

On the day that Daisy was foiled at the Stuffs', Cassian was sitting on a deck chair between two piles of coal, wiping his hands on a piece of cotton waste and thinking about low-pressure condensers, when he had a most peculiar sensation. It was as if someone were shining a flashlight at him, but a flashlight emitting no beam of visible light. When he looked up, he saw the chief engineer's eyes, not whirling anymore, but fixed upon him.

Cassian raised a hand and gave a sort of salute.

The chief winked.

Cassian got up and strolled among the coal heaps to the control shed. Using a bit of stick he had in his pocket, he pressed the brass bell. The door opened immediatly. "Comming in," said the chief. "You haf big mechanical aptitude, I am thinking. Cuppy tea?"

"Don't mind if I do," said Cassian, looking around.

There were colossal banks of switches, whole families of brass wheels of all sizes, gauges and dials, and something that looked like a model *Kleptomanic* beetling steadily across a sea of mercury. And there were the clocks, dozens of them, arranged by type, ticking out a frenzied cross-rhythm.

The two of them exchanged engine gossip for five minutes. Then the engineer took an iron teapot and held it under a brass tap. Boiling water roared in. The engineer let it brew, then poured one cup, added condensed milk, and passed it to Cassian. "Aren't you having one?" said Cassian.

The eyes gave a small whirl. "I hates tea," said the engineer.

"Delicious," said Cassian, sipping.

"Delicious things also I hate," said the chief.

Cassian raised a polite eyebrow, wondering if there were any biscuits.

"I am hating just about everything," said the chief. "I am hating first the schtarting-up valves here, zen ze regulators, zen ze valve controllers, and ze bearing oiler monitor gauges—"

"Would you mind repeating that?" said Cassian slyly.

"Ja, I vould!" cried the chief. "You are coming in here for

tea, not to learn ship-schtarting procedure. I hate ship-schtarting procedure," he said. The eyes were definitely whirling again. "Plus, I hate captain, crew, burglars, schtokers, my clothes, my feet, myself, damn rewolution, people, everything."

"Ah," said Cassian, noting the sulky jut of the chief's lower lip and realizing that any child with half-decent nanny training could provoke a really spectacular tantrum here with no trouble at all. It would not be clever, of course. But once Cassian had discovered how something worked, he could seldom resist starting it up. He pointed to the bear's head in the glass case. "So I suppose you hate the Royal Edward, too?"

"*Noooooooo!*" roared the chief. "*I lof him! He iss my bear! Smellink good and kind, so kind!*"

"So if someone found the rest of him and put him back together?"

"I vurship this person. I do vot he vant forever and ever."

"Jolly good," said Cassian. He looked at his watch. "Gosh, is that the time? Thanks for the tea, Chief."

"Is nodings," said the chief. "How I hates it, zis tea."

As Cassian left, all the cuckoo clocks went off at once.

"We have got to get those bear bits for the chief," said Daisy.

"Why?" said Primrose.

"Because we can't stay alongside forever," said Cassian.

"Why not?" said Primrose.

"Because it's a ship, and ships are supposed to move around the world."

"Not necessarily," said Primrose. "I'm quite happy. So's Chef."

"Have you ever asked yourself," said Daisy, "where the food comes from?"

"Out of the larder," said Primrose. "I'm not stupid, you know."

"Quite the reverse," said Daisy tactfully. "But it's not quite as simple as that—"

"Daisy, you are right: it is an awesome burden of responsibility," said a new voice. It belonged to Nanny Pete, who had wandered into the warm place by number-two funnel where the Darlings were sitting. "There's only three of us nannies active now. Great burden on us, really. Don't know how long we can go on."

"Nanny burglary isn't the only way. What's wrong with breaking and entering?" said Cassian.

"And mugging and ram raiding?" said Daisy.

"Haven't got the heart for it somehow," said Pete. "Fair to say that most of the people here are your kinder type of burglar. Then you kids demonstrated unto one and all the skills of civilization, like, and well, it's frightening, really."

"You mean it's our fault?"

"It is merely," said Pete, "that everyone thought we were vicious and villainous and similar. But since you came on board, we realize we are mere amateurs and you are the real thing."

"How very gratifying," said Daisy, blushing pink.

"I should say so," said Primrose.

"One feels very humble," said Cassian.

"But we got a problem," said Pete Fryer. "We are in need of the bits of the bear them builders have got, and the problem is, how to get 'em."

"Just what we were saying. But the captain will know," said Daisy.

"Um, ye-es," said Pete. "Which is to say, of course she will."

"So how?" said Cassian.

"Challenge, probably," said Pete.

"Challenge?"

"'Scuse me," said Pete. "I've got to go. Plus, it's past your wood bird."

"I beg your pardon?"

"Woodshed, bed. Bird lime, time."

"Ah. Goodness me!" said Daisy, checking her watch. "So it is!"

And off they went, good as gold.

Later, they lay in their gilded beds, watching the silver disk of the moon shining through the portholes. "You know what?" said Cassian. "Something's funny."

Primrose said, "If you ask me, everything's funny."

"What do you mean?" said Daisy.

"When did the Bear's Bum come into the nursery?"

"Always been there," said Primrose.

"No," said Daisy. "You were born. But you were just a baby. Too young to notice much."

"Was not," said Primrose.

"Were!" said Cassian.

"Was—"

"Children!" cried Daisy, in a voice like the snap of a nanny's knicker elastic. "What are you getting at, Cassian?"

"It's just odd, that's all," said Cassian. "I mean, I think it turned up at about the same time as Secretary Mummy."

"After Real Mummy left, then."

"I suppose so. Odd."

"What?"

"That whole tombola business. I mean, clever of the captain to notice who was bidding."

"It's not the sort of thing you'd forget in a hurry," said Daisy.

"You know how they go on," said Primrose. "Secretary Mummy, f'rinstance. Oh yes, it was a lovely evening. Lady Mortdarthur and Lord Cringe were there, and Lord Cringe said, 'Look at that roast peacock: I'm going to eat it all up,' and Lady Peachbottom laughed so much I thought she would burst, ha, ha, ha!"

"Ha, ha, ha," said Cassian gloomily.

"Ha," said Daisy. Her sister was right, of course. "I don't care," she said.

"Best not think about it," said Cassian.

"Exactly," said Primrose. "The main thing is to get our hands on the bits of the bear. I'll sew them up." Daisy and Cassian nodded in the dark. Primrose's sewing was nearly as magical as her cooking. "Then off we go!"

"Off we go," said Daisy.

"Over the far horizon," said Cassian. "But first assemble your bear." There was a silence, during which the moonbeams continued to fall on the brocade counterpanes. "What do you think a challenge is?"

"Not challenge, Challenge," said Daisy.

"No idea," said Primrose.

Silence descended on the cabin. Then there was the odd snore. Then there was more silence. Then it was morning.

"Hoop ha and hee!" cried Primrose, soaping up a storm in the gigantic bath. "And what will today hold?"

"Plenty," said Cassian.

And of course he was dead right.

Breakfast was an ingenious blend of porridge with ample maple syrup, Parma ham omelettes, and tropical fruits. Much refreshed, the Darlings went about their daily business—Daisy to the ready-nanny room, Primrose to the kitchens, and Cassian to the engine room—familiar worlds, all of them.

But all of them seemed subtly to have changed. As she went to the ready-nanny room, Daisy was surprised to see a blur in the distance, a blur that turned out not to be in the distance at all but just to look like it, because of its minute size. Actually it was Nosy Clanger, skipping with such speed that the rope was a silvery fuzz like a bumblebee's wings.

"What are you doing?" said Daisy, highly nanny.

"Falt, pepper, muftard, binegar," said Nosy with fearful rapidity. "Playin' nifely on me own, N. Daify."

"Ah," said Daisy, and went on her way, frowning.

Primrose was in the early stages of developing a biscuit known as Angel Devil Dream Surprise. Needing advice on the icing, she threaded her way through the stoves to visit her friend Sophie Nickit, who had spent the last week on a replica of the Sistine Chapel, ceiling and all, in sugar. But Sophie had left the chapel aside for the moment. She had replaced her svelte roller gear with unpleasant gray warm-ups and was whipping a batter.

"What is it?" said Primrose.

"Heavy cake," said Sophie, with a grim set to her pretty jaw.

"But why?" said Primrose.

"When the going gets tough, the tough get going," said Sophie. And would say no more.

Cassian arrived in the engine room to find the chief engineer sitting in the control room in a golden chair. The chief's arms were folded. Over his head was a badly painted placard, bearing the word WON'T.

"Won't what?" said Cassian.

The chief pressed a button. The sign rotated. On the other side was written the word SHAN'T. The door slammed. Cassian sighed and went off to re-grind the number-two oil-cooler thrust-bearing bearing plate. On the way, he heard a swifter hammering noise, as of an engine. But Cassian knew all the *Kleptomanic*'s engines, and he had not heard this one before. So he went to investigate.

The hammering was not an engine. It came from Giant Luggage's fists. What Giant Luggage was hitting was a huge sack of coal, hung from an overhead girder. There was a hole in the sack, from which dribbled a stream of fine coal dust as Luggage beat the lumps to powder. There was quite a pile there.

"What are you doing?" said Cassian.

"Hur, hur," said Giant Luggage, grinning bashfully.

Well, the man had been breaking coal. But why with his fists and not the hammers provided? And why to useless slack? Cassian was about to inquire further, because he liked to get to the bottom of things. But suddenly a fearful rhythmic squawking came from the loudspeaker. *"Alert,"* said the metallic voice. *"Five-alarm nanny emergency. Giant luggage, Cassian, and duty nannies to the launchpad, clean, and that means behind yer ears an' all. Drive, drive, drive."*

Cassian and Giant Luggage began to run.

"Daisy," said the captain at the end of the briefing. "I am putting you in overall command of this operation. It is the last chunk of the Edward, and we need it desperately."

"But we can't just turn up," said Daisy. "They haven't asked us. You know what nannies are like. Territorial. Like wolverines."

"I gave this one a ring," said the captain. "Yesterday."

"Oh?"

"Bit of a one for the horses, Nanny Magnum," said the captain. "I gave her a tip. Suggested she pinch Lady Smarte's tiara, pawn it, and put the proceeds on a horse called Staggery Jack for the two-forty race at Lunchestown."

"But how did you know Staggery Jack wouldn't win?"

"They almost never do," said Pete. "Plus your sister cooked up a batch of Slow Bran for the horse, and we sent Pygmy Eric over disguised as a stable lad, and he fed the horse the bran, and Bob's your mother's brother."

"We hardly remember our mother," said Daisy sadly.

"Ah, well," said the captain, laying a hand on her shoulder. "Into each life a little rain must fall, and she has my sympathy. But the important thing is, it is now four-thirty p.m., and Staggery Jack is still running, and the rest of the horses are tucked up nicely in their boxes, and Nanny Magnum has had a bit of a breakdown, and you are in like Flint."

"Flint?" said Daisy.

"Sort of stone," said the captain vaguely. "Oh, look, here come the rest of the Elite Squad. Off you go now and Godspeed!"

Cassian smelled slightly of soap, but he was still covered in engine oil; not that there was anything unusual in that or anything anyone could do about it. "It's the Big One," said Daisy.

"Whuh?"

"Smarte Castle. The last limb of the Edward, or to be more precise, the torso. Our chance to draw level. It's not going to be easy, the captain says. So we're the senior team."

Cassian looked at the reflection in the Jag's gleaming black flank. Four figures. Four pairs of brogues, four pairs of thick stockings, four brown nanny dresses with white aprons, four stiff collars, four brown overcoats, four bowler hats.

They climbed into the Jag. It swung down to the quay, Nosy Clanger gibbering at them from the netting. Giant Luggage was driving, Nanny Pete in the rumble seat. Luggage gunned the engine. The Jag purred through the sliding doors and into the Port Quarter.

"Here they come," said Cassian.

And sure enough, onto their tail, three blocks back, had turned a huge, rust-splotched white van.

"Go slow," said Daisy.

"Hur, hur," said Giant Luggage, lifting his size-eighteen accelerator foot. The Jag slowed. The white van slowed, too. They crawled in procession out of town.

"What happens now?" said Daisy.

"The big-end bearings on that van go, by the sound of it." Cassian took out a small notebook. "What do they keep in it?" he said.

"Digger. Dozer. Dumper."

Cassian's pen scuttled over the page, doing sums. "Thirty-eight tons, velocity of light, mass at center, expansion of the universe, let pi be 3.14, well, good enough. . . . Where's the nearest tree?"

They were in the country now. "There," said Daisy, perhaps a little tetchily. Really, Cassian could be so lazy sometimes. Could he not find his own trees?

"Wrong kind," said Cassian, tetchy himself.

"Here we are," said Nanny Pete. "Smarte Castle."

"Hur, hur," said Giant Luggage, four-wheel drifting the Jag between two marble pillars with lions on top.

The van seemed to be speeding up. Daisy thought it might have crushing on its mind. "What are you going to do?" she said.

Cassian's forehead looked faintly sweaty. "Is there a river?" he said. "An ornamental bridge, perhaps?"

"No ornamental bridge," said Pete. "No river."

"It'll have to be trees, then," said Cassian. The drive went through a wood. "Slow," he said. A track turned off to the right. "Down the track."

Giant Luggage swung the wheel. The Jag turned onto the track. The white van followed, roaring and belching smoke, its radiator grinning a rust-flecked grin that filled the rearview mirror. The trees closed in on either side. "He's catching up," said Daisy, panicky. Then—

"He's stopped."

"Not stopped," said Cassian. "Stuck."

And when she looked round, there was the white van, firmly jammed between two oak trees.

"Nice driving, Luggage," said Cassian.

"Hur, hur," said Giant Luggage, giving the van a cheery wave out of the window. The white van waved back. Not cheerily, and not with a hand. Nastily. With a digger bucket.

"He's using it on the trees," said Cassian. "He'll be out of there soon. Floor it, Luggage."

Luggage floored it. The Jag hurtled onto a long, straight drive across a rolling park with deer. The turrets of Smarte Castle rose ahead. There was a puff of smoke on the battlements, and something whizzed over the Jag's roof. "Stone me," said Nanny Pete. "Someone's shooting at us. With a cannon."

Daisy's lips were a tight line. "Handguns are naughty but neat," she said. "Machine guns are wicked but sometimes understandable. But cannons are nasty and messy and inaccurate and thoroughly unspeakable. I do absolutely draw the line at cannons. Stop the car."

She got out and marched across the drawbridge and under the arch. From the battlements, childish eyes watched her suspiciously. A butler in a striped waistcoat opened the huge, nail-studded door. The shadows swallowed her up.

"There," said Nanny Pete, "goes a brave little woman."

Hefting his socket set, Cassian trotted after his sister. Something told him she would be needing backup. Giant Luggage parked the Jag behind a handy bunker. Then he and Nanny Pete crammed their hats over their ears, scooped up their swag bags, and went in, too.

The inside of Smarte Castle was as Daisy had expected—snooty butler, stags' horns on the walls, diamond-crusted fire irons twinkling in a vast fireplace. "Miss Henrietta is in the nursery," said the butler, down his nose. "Master Arthur is on the west battlements. Her ladyship asks me to remind you that Master Arthur is a delicate child in need of constant love and attention. His shooting at people with cannons should be interpreted as a cry for help."

"And when will her ladyship be back?"

"Her ladyship did not say," said the butler. "Her ladyship and his lordship have naffed off to Scotland to chase wild animals. It normally takes a month or so. Sometimes longer."

"Ah."

"And if I might venture the observation," said the butler, "good luck, cocky, you are going to need it. They took Nanny Magnum off to the mental home at four sharp this afternoon and the shooting started straight after; need I say more?"

"I like a child with spirit," said Daisy. "Which way to the nursery?"

At the second landing, the stair carpet covering changed from thick Turkish carpet to linoleum. At the third, there were bare boards underfoot, and the air had that familiar soap pong. From behind a white door came the sound of someone practicing scales on a piano. Daisy went in.

As she had guessed, it was the nursery. There were generations of teddy bear portraits on the walls and pictures of sweet children in flowery meadows, wearing puff skirts and velvet shorts and clean white ankle socks. Daisy and Cassian came to a halt.

There was a glass case containing something that looked like a moldy bag of sawdust. The torso (realized Daisy, with bumping heart) of the Royal Edward.

At the piano sat a girl in a neat frock, with perfectly brushed hair in a blue velvet Alice band. Her socks were easily as white as the ones in the pictures on the walls. They matched her face.

"Nana!" she cried, bursting into a watery simper.

"You will be Henrietta," said Daisy. "Hetty for short? Or is it Etta?"

"Just Henrietta," she said, and pursed her lips primly. "Thank goodness you are here. I would like to tell on Arthur. I know he is delicate, but that is no excuse for blowing people up with cannons. I am shocked and so was Nanny Magnum, but she has gone and I do not understand why. Soon it will be time for high tea."

"Nana will burn you some custard, then," said Daisy.

The whey-faced idiot clapped. "Goody!" she cried.

Cassian said, "But why do you like burnt custard?"

"Because it is good for me!" The girl stared at Daisy like a dog expecting a bone.

"Good girl," said Daisy, wincing. "Now let us hear you practice your scales."

The clean little fingers plodded up and down the keyboard,

slowly, boringly, not rushing, not making a mistake. Cassian said, "I may be sick."

"Shame on you!" hissed Daisy. She rushed into the nursery kitchen and rustled up a dose of peaches and ice cream and unburnt custard from among the champagne bottles and caviar tins in the fridge that said NANNIES ONLY—TOUCH AND DIE. It only took three minutes.

Henrietta ate the lot. "That was delicious," she said brightly. Then her face dulled. "But there was something wrong with it."

"Not burnt?" said Daisy.

Henrietta shrugged, confused, nearly in tears.

"What about eat-what-you-are-given?" said Daisy.

"But it tasted good!"

"In future, send back anything that doesn't."

Henrietta's lip began to quiver.

"You just have to put your foot down," said Daisy.

"But they make you stand in the corner. Kneel on dried peas. Go to bed without your supper. I couldn't."

"Try."

But Henrietta had begun to practice her scales again, slow, boring, mind-shatteringly loud.

"Listen," said Daisy. "You don't have to do what you're told—"

"La, la, la," sang Henrietta. "Not listenin'!"

The sudden bang of a cannon rattled the windows. Daisy

took the torso off the wall, walked out of the nursery, and closed the door quietly on the thundering scales within. "Too far gone," she said. "It happens."

Giant Luggage stood twisting his bowler hat into a pretzel. "We can't just leave the poor mite," said Pete, horrified.

"We have to," said Daisy. "She's doing what she was told to do. She causes no trouble. A nice, quiet child."

"But that's diabolical," said Pete.

"That's nannies," said Daisy. "Have you learned nothing?"

"The battlements!" said Cassian.

The door onto the battlements was locked. Daisy had expected no less. "Well?" she said to Cassian, who had followed.

"We could use a chain saw, but that would be rather noisy," he said. "And he'll have the door covered."

Pete said, "Luggage'll soup it."

"Soup?"

But Luggage was already dripping a clear liquid gingerly into the keyhole. "Nitroglycerine," said Pete.

"Hur, hur," said Luggage. He lit a fuse, straightened up, and put his sausage fingers into his cauliflower ears.

"Light blue touch paper and retire immediately," said Pete.

There was a colossal explosion. Cassian and Giant Luggage sprinted through the smoke, keeping low.

On the roof a small child stood by an ancient cannon.

The child was wearing a lace collar, velvet knickerbockers, white silk stockings, and buckle shoes and aiming a cross-bow at Luggage's midsection. Luggage made sentimental noises, sidestepping a bolt. He stretched out gigantic, welcoming arms.

The child began to snivel, knuckling its lovely blue eyes. Daisy said, "Look out—"

But it was too late. Giant Luggage had stepped up to the infant and patted its golden curls. Quick as a cobra, the infant sank its teeth into the side of Luggage's hand.

"Aargh!" cried Luggage, shaking his hand, to which the child was still attached.

"Oi!" said Cassian to the infant. "Arthur or whatever your name is. Stop thrashing about like that and I will show you how to lay this cannon, because that shooting you were doing before was actually embarrassing."

"Was not!" shrieked the child. But in order to shriek, it opened its mouth, and its teeth came out of Giant Luggage's hand, and Giant Luggage lurched back, bleeding.

"Look at this," said Cassian, ramming in powder, wad, ball, and new wad and priming the touch hole with gunpowder from the horn provided. "Got your crosswind, right?"

"Course," said the child, sulky but listening now.

"Plus your elevation."

"Teach your grandmother to suck eggs."

"But have you got your humidity?"

There was a short but well-filled silence. Then Arthur said, "Humidity?"

Cassian shook his head wearily. "Crucial," he said. "Now forgive me, but if we were to want to hit . . . say, that white van coming toward the castle at one hundred and ten miles per hour, how would you do it?"

"Ten degrees depression," said the child. "Lay off one-point-three degrees for breeze."

"Is that it?"

"Course it is."

"Nope," said Cassian. "Plus up one for humidity. Now do it. Fire."

The cannon boomed. A large hole appeared in the center of the white van's radiator. The white van slewed into the moat. Figures emerged, swimming clumsily. They struggled up the bank, staggered across the drawbridge, and began hammering on the door.

"And nobody hurt," said Cassian.

"Awwwww," said the child, disappointed.

"What shall we do?" said Daisy.

"Oh, I'll take care of them," said Arthur. "Got a light?" Luggage gave him some matches. He kindled a fire under a large cauldron of oil standing by a gully. "Fried builder," he said. "Very unhealthy."

Daisy was most impressed. All children needed to make them happy and fulfilled was a little encouragement. She realized that this child's sister was in safe hands. She said, "Is there a back entrance? Because I think you can take care of all this yourself."

"I think I can," said the child, simpering. "Thanks for that stuff about humidity; it'll come in handy. By the way, you're not real nannies, are you?"

They stared at him.

"Only it's all round the county. You ring up emergency nannies and your house gets knocked down and everything gets stolen. But do swipe what you like on the way out. There's a Rolls-Royce in the garage. I'll get the Jag back to you later, if I can. And if you see the coppers, tell them you're with Lord Arthur Smarte, and they'll leave you alone."

"Yes," they said, dazed. "We will."

Luggage and Pete wandered around the castle, doing a little looting. Then they proceeded to the garage, where the Rolls was waiting, as advertised. Daisy laid the Edward's torso tenderly on the backseat and climbed in. The great car whispered out into the park and away.

"What a delightful child," said Daisy as they drove through the police roadblock, waving regally. "And frankly, what a hideous bit of bear." She held it up in front of her: a beige lump, loosely tacked to its shield. "Lot of fuss about very little, really."

"About a lot," said Cassian.

Daisy tossed the shield onto the seat. Something rolled

out of it and bounced on the carpet. Daisy picked it up, put it in her pocket, and forgot all about it.

"Pity about the Jag," said Cassian.

Giant Luggage said nothing. He was looking at his bitten hand. It was red and angry, and it hurt. It hurt a lot.

"Dear little Arthur," said Daisy as the derrick swung the Rolls off the quay. "And his sister, so sweet."

Cassian was getting rather bored with the way Daisy was going on. This nanny thing was all very well, but nannies were the enemy, and more and more often nowadays she seemed to be turning into one. He heard Pete say, "How's the hand, Luggage?"

"Hur," said Luggage, gnawing an agonized lip, and Pete frowned, looking worried.

Something was going on.

The wheelbarrow men came. There were a couple of barrows of jeweled household stuff, bellows, fish slices, nothing much.

"Luggage!" cried the loudspeaker. "Training!"

"Hurrrr!" cried Luggage, springing toward the gym deck. As he ran (clumsily, thought Daisy; a great lack of deportment), he tapped his hand against the door frame. "Aaargh!" he shrieked, clutching his wrist.

With one swift stride, Daisy was at his elbow. "Show Nana," she said.

"Grunt," said Luggage.

"I shan't ask again," said Daisy.

The hand came out. The red-spotted handkerchief came off.

"Just as I thought," said Daisy, tutting. "Really, I wonder when little Arthur last cleaned his teeth!"

"Hur," said Luggage. "Eek!"

For Daisy had prodded him again. "It's antibiotics for you, Master Luggage, and a week in a sling," she said.

"Grunt," said Luggage.

Daisy pursed her lips. She said, "Be off with you now, and do what Nana says."

"Daisy," said Cassian after Luggage had lumbered sheepishly away, "you're not yourself."

"Stuff and nonsense." Her chin was up, her lips compressed, her eyes glassy. Cassian thought she looked . . . weird. He went into the wheelhouse and took the top off the kitchen voice pipe. Five minutes later, Primrose came on deck. She said, "Drink this."

"My name is Nana," said Daisy, in a strange, high voice. "You will please mind your p's and q's. Children should be seen and not heard. A cup of tea is sometimes very welcome." She took a deep draught. Then she coughed and spluttered. "Ork!" she cried. "What is this?"

"Pepsi Brown Cow. Pepsi and ice cream."

"Where am I?" said Daisy. The glassy look had gone from her eyes.

"You were nearly lost in Nanny World. Now, men, hat off, and get the rest of the Brown Cow down you. It'll make all the difference."

"Sigh," said Daisy, downing the dregs of the delicious non-nanny drink. "That's better."

"Thought you were gone for a moment there," said Primrose.

"Yeah. Thanks." Daisy made a face. "It was that girl Henrietta. And bowler hats . . . After a while, they just start to bend your mind. Remember Elsie?"

"Sure we remember Elsie."

Elsie had been a kindly girl who worked in the kitchen at Number One, Avenue Marshal Posh. She had always been ready to smuggle out the chocolates the ambassador refused to eat when he came to drinks. Then Nanny Hatchett had asked her to be sub-nanny. And as soon as the bowler hat had settled on her brow, she had started rapping out orders. She had knitted a really embarrassing baby hat for Primrose, tried to get Cassian out of welding and into Legos, and read aloud to Daisy from *Peter Pan,* which made Daisy actually sick. She had finally left in a hail of fire and was now bringing up some little warlords and warladies on a mountain somewhere.

"It's definitely the hat," said Daisy. She cast hers to the deck and stamped on it with her brogue.

"Morning, all," said a voice. They looked up and saw the captain: a new, different captain, wearing a neat tailored suit and shoes with high heels. "Sick of your hat?"

"A bit," said Daisy, shamefaced.

"Responsibilities," said the captain, sighing. "They can get on top of you." She looked tired under the makeup.

"Well, we've got the torso," said Daisy, driven by a strange urge to cheer up this peculiar but nice person.

"Marvelous work," said the captain, with a strangely preoccupied air.

"Is everything all right?" said Cassian.

"Fine, fine," said the captain, waving an exquisite hand.

Daisy frowned. Things were clicking in her mind. "So the chief's got the head of the Edward. And you've got half the rest," she said. "And the builders have got the other half."

"Quite," said the captain, giving her a smile that combined dazzlement with a sort of wistful sadness.

"How are you going to get the other half?"

"Oh, well . . ." said the captain.

Daisy's spine stiffened. "Speak up!" she cried. "Spit it out! Tell the truth!"

"Daisy!" said Cassian, shocked.

"Sorry. Relapse," said Daisy, her brow glistening with sweat. "It's got to be a Challenge, hasn't it?"

"A Challenge?" said the captain.

"Speak up!" cried Daisy. "Spit it out! Tell—"

"Yes, yes, yes," said the captain wearily. "Yes. All right. It's a Challenge."

"Please explain."

The captain looked astonished. "Don't tell me you've never heard of it?"

"Hardly."

The captain sighed. "Well, I don't know what they teach you nowadays, I really don't. It's in the Statutes of Larceny of the Worshipful Company of Burglars, Smash and Grabbers, Financial Service Engineers and Allied Trades. To settle questions of ownership. Basically, it's trial by single combat."

"Wow," said Cassian, impressed. "Like witches holding bits of red-hot iron and if they blister, they're witches and if they don't, they aren't?"

"Teacher's pet," said the captain reprovingly. "Nobody likes a know-all, and besides, you are thinking of trial by ordeal. But basically, yes. You have a champion from each side. They fight, with a police referee, on the challenger's manor. Winner takes all. In this case, the missing parts of the Edward, and hence the loyalty of the chief."

"Hence all this training," said Cassian. "Great!"

"You don't understand!" said the captain. "My burglars are so sweet and kind and gentle. They abhor violence except in the line of duty."

Daisy tched. "They nicked plenty of gear," she said.

"But if we lose . . ." said the captain.

"We won't," said Daisy.

"Leave that to us," said Cassian. "Who's the champion?"

"Giant Luggage."

"He wouldn't hurt a fly."

"Yes, he would," said Daisy. "I've seen him. He cried afterward, but Primrose can fix that. I'll go and deliver this challenge, never fear. They won't hurt me."

"Probably not," said the captain faintly. "Oh, I did so hope it wouldn't come to this."

"No use crying over spilt milk," said Daisy.

"Daisy!" said Primrose.

"Sorry. Now, then, I'll need a driver for the Rolls. And you can tell me the rules."

"And I," said Cassian, "will need an elite corps of engineers and five burglars who can stoke boilers and twenty with dock experience."

"What for?" said the captain.

"When we beat the builders and reassemble the Royal Edward for the chief, do you want to hang around?"

"Of course not."

"Well, then," said Cassian.

"And it would be nice if you could give me four dozen eggs, some sugar, red wine, stinking hellebore, and one hundred and twenty grams of toad warts," said Primrose. "Oh, and a needle and thread."

"Of course," said the captain. "But why?"

The children pursed their lips, nanny style. "You'll just have to wait and see," they said.

Hilda the Builder put the fifth sugar into her tea and stirred, wheezing a little with the effort. Outside the window, a gray drizzle was falling on the yard—several hectares of rusty diggers and mixers, tumbled piles of concrete blocks, and a bungalow someone had started building and changed his mind about halfway. In the middle of the yard, a long black car had just cruised to a halt. Hilda said, "Wozzat, Dan?"

White Van Dan looked up from his copy of *Daily Girls*. He was a wiry little person with a monkey face and tattoos all the way up his arms, so he looked like an ape wearing a skintight suit of ladies in bikinis. "Woz wot?" he said.

"The car."

"The Roller?"

"Yeh."

"He's stopped."

"I can see he's stopped."

The Roller door opened, and a small figure climbed out. She wore a brown bowler hat, a long brown overcoat, and brown wool stockings. Her lips were pressed together in disgust as she picked her way between the puddles and the drifts of old burger boxes.

"Oozis?" said Hilda the Builder, swallowing a Mars bar whole.

"Search me," said Dan.

It was Daisy, of course.

The caravan was green with mold. Black smoke oozed from its stovepipe, smelling of burning plastic. A sign over the door said D+H HIGH-CLASS BUILDERS. The sign was tilted to the left, because the nails that attached it to the caravan had come out, because they were too short and had been hammered in wrong. Daisy splashed through the last black puddle and opened the rickety door. "Mr. Dan?" she said.

The wiry little man smiled, a smile that lit up his sharp white teeth and his gold identity bracelet and watch but not his eyes, which were gray as cement.

"And you must be Miss Hilda," she said. "How d'you do?"

The huge woman in filthy decorator's overalls frowned blubberily at the roll of foam-backed carpet she was feeding into the stove. There were full ashtrays and dirty teacups everywhere. The ceiling was varnished brown with the grease of many fry-ups.

"This," said Daisy, "is absolutely revolting."

White Van Dan had been edging round behind her to cut off her line of retreat. Now he froze. "What did you say?"

"You should be ashamed of yourself," said Daisy, through tight lips. "This is disgusting. It is quite unnecessary to live like pigs." She put her hand in her overcoat pocket. Dan's hand went into his pocket, too, and his eyes narrowed. But Daisy's hand came out slowly, holding a long brown envelope with a red crest on the flap. "Read this," she said. "I suppose you *can* read?"

Dan snatched it out of Daisy's hand and scowled at it angrily. "What is it?" he said.

"It is what we call writing," said Daisy sweetly. "Words are made of letters. The one with a dot on top is *i*. For *idiot*. That one is *f*. For *fool*—"

"I can read," said Dan, rending the envelope.

"He can, too," said Hilda, admiringly. "And nearly write an' all."

"So what shall I tell them?" said Daisy.

"About what?"

Daisy tutted and sighed, casting her eyes at the ceiling in an exceptionally annoying way. "This is a Challenge," she said. "The AAA Aardvark Nanny Agency presents its compliments—"

"Langwidge," said Hilda.

"—and invites White Van Dan and Firm to select a champion to fight its own champion on board SS *Kleptomanic* tomorrow or other convenient date, for possession of the opposition's bits of the Royal Edward, winner take all. Usual rules apply."

"Fight?" said Dan. "No way."

"Fraidy cat," said Daisy.

"Am not," said Dan.

"Is not," said Hilda.

"Are. Prove it."

"What," said Dan, "is stopping me dropping you in a great big pit of wet cement?"

"Don't be an utter baby," said Daisy, nose high. "Shall we say after tea tomorrow?"

"Too right, toffee nose," said Dan. "We'll be using Dickie the Brickie."

"Toffee nose," said Hilda, getting the idea. "Toff—"

"Sticks and stones may break my bones, but words will never hurt me," said Daisy, and walked briskly through the drizzle to the Roller.

Hilda watched the great car glide silently away. She spooned extra sugar into her tea for the sake of her nerves.

"Cheek," said Dan.

"Cheek," said Hilda.

When they went out later to play with the bulldozer, they saw that near where the Roller had stood, an expanse of cement, wet earlier in the day, was covered in writing. HILDA IS A *, it read. But the * was not a *. In the cement, rock hard now, was the imprint of an enormous bottom.

"Ooh," said Hilda. "Nasty."

"Not as nasty as us," said Dan. "You wait."

"You sure?"

"I'm always sure," said Dan.

"But you were sure you could mend the van," said Hilda.

"I am sure that when we get their chief engineer, he will be able to mend the van and build us a better one. And we can start up again in Iceland," said Dan.

"Oh," said Hilda.

"Say, 'Brilliant, Dan,'" said Dan.

"Brilliant, Dan."

"Oh, I dunno," said Dan, blushing.

Back on the *Kleptomanic,* the burglars were in a state of huge excitement. Quite a lot of these tattooed and hardened geezers had secretly thought it undignified to go around dressed up as nannies. A good fight would make everyone feel much better. The training became intense. Ancient sacks were stuffed with ancient life jackets, hung from chandeliers, and pummeled until the dust hung in fat gray clouds. Ancient mooring lines were pressed into service as skipping ropes. All day long, Daisy and the captain sat on the bridge, treating a succession of black eyes and bleeding noses and skinned knuckles.

"Tell me," said Daisy when they were alone for a moment. "What makes you think that when the Firm lose the fight, they will stop causing trouble?"

"There are ancient traditions at work here," said the captain. "I feel sure that the Firm will respect them, and that their better nature will prevail."

"Really?"

The captain started filing her nails with anxious vigor. "No," she said. "Actually, not really, not at all. Sometimes I feel that we are too trusting, creatures from a kinder, older time. No smash, you know. And only the tiniest bit of grab."

After lunch, one of the voice pipes peeped. "Cap'n," said the voice. "The Contender is doing his public training, should you be interested."

"Extremely," said the captain. "Come along, Daisy."

A space had been cleared in the middle of the gym. A large punching bag hung from the ceiling. By the bag stood Giant Luggage, like a sack of bowling balls, wearing knee-length shorts and boxing gloves.

"We are ready," said the captain.

"Hur, hur," said Luggage with a nervous half smile. In Daisy's view, the smile fell some distance short of the saber-toothed grin of an assassin.

"Train, ho!" cried Nanny Pete, stopwatch in hand, dancing from foot to foot in a sweat suit and trainers.

Luggage launched himself on the bag and started to pound it with horrid vigor.

Actually, with not very horrid vigor.

After ten seconds he stopped. "Hur," he said in a small voice. He pushed the bag away from him with a large, disgusted shove, turned round, and faced the captain, spreading his hands, fumbling with the laces of his right glove.

The bag swung back and smote him on the back of the head. He went down like a building.

There was an awful silence.

Then Pete was on his knees by the body, taking off the right glove. And there was Luggage's main punching hand, red, large, and horribly painful, thanks to the unbrushed teeth of Lord Arthur Smarte.

Daisy frowned. "Off games for a week," she said.

"But—"

"It is not a good sign," said Daisy, "when the challenger is knocked out by his own training equipment."

That was true, of course.

"Very well," said the captain. "Substitute procedure initiated, if you please. Nanny Pete?"

"It would be a kebab."

"I beg your pardon?"

"Kebab, doner, honor," said Pete, eyes twinkling and chest swelling visibly.

"Ah," said the captain, reeling a little. "Well, be that as it may, congratulations. You are our new champion."

Daisy and the captain returned to the bridge. "Dear Pete," said the captain. "But perhaps too kind and not really big enough for a champion. Dickie the Brickie is . . . well, a behemoth."

"What?" said Primrose.

"A monster. As in very big and very ugly."

"Relax," said Daisy. "Everything is under control."

The captain looked anxious. "Do you think so?"

"Leave it to us," said Daisy, and explained.

When she had finished, the captain was still looking anxious. "It's a bold plan," she said. "Daring, I grant you. But are you sure it will work?"

"We were brought up by nannies," said Daisy. "Real nannies. With respect, you burglars have had it easy."

"*Such* a comfort," said the captain, hugging her. "Daisy, you are *perfect*."

"One does one's best to do one's bit," said Daisy awkwardly. "Now, I must pop off and make plans."

She went. Watching her trim, sturdy figure march about its business, the captain brushed away a tear.

She had become most attached to Daisy. It was just another thing to worry about.

There were so many.

A bit later, the Darlings were having a meeting in the suite.

"Everyone clear?" said Daisy.

"Sorted," said Primrose.

"As crystal," said Cassian.

"Background, please," said Daisy.

"They were talking about the substitute procedure in the kitchen," said Primrose. "By the terms of the Parkhurst Convention, Dickie the Brickie is blindfolded. He comes onto the ship. In the absence of the nominated champion, he gets to fight the first person he sees when they take the blindfold off him."

"And if it's the ship's cat?"

"It'll make a change from mice. But it is accepted that the captain sets things up so the first person he sees is a good challenger."

"Good. So what have you been doing?"

"Cooking." Primrose smiled shyly. "I think it'd be best if Dickie lost the fight."

"Oh, I dunno," said Cassian.

"What?" shrieked both his sisters at once.

"Life moves on," said Cassian irritatingly.

So of course Daisy told him he had a smudge of oil on his nose and asked him why he was so dirty. And he smiled a superior smile.

"Up to something," said Primrose. "Definitely."

"Mischief, I'll be bound," said Daisy.

"Daisy!"

"Oops. Sorry. Any more nanny stuff, put a bucket of water over me."

"With pleasure!" said Primrose and Cassian together.

"Anyway," said Daisy, "we stand on the brink of a new and strange world. Our first home has been flattened by burglars. Our parents have vanished. We are in the power of a self-professed lady burglar, delightful, I grant you, but a woman of unknown motives. And even now our new home is in the balance. Everything may be won or lost on the slug of a criminal fist. This time tomorrow, who knows? We may be engineerless, running from the vengeance of the white van, or triumphant. It will be strange and lonely and rootless. It will, in short, be dead weird."

"Fantastic!" said Primrose.

"Wonderful!" cried Cassian.

"Quite so!" said Daisy. "Now, onward!"

14

The day of the big fight dawned bright and clear. The Rules of Challenge had been agreed upon and, as per routine, signed in blood by both parties. Nanny Pete Fryer's selection as champion had been a move popular with the burglars, who had said he was a diamond and given him three hearty cheers. Giant Luggage was rattling with powerful antibiotics. Half an hour before fight time Pete was on the Jag deck, dressed in satin shorts, killing time by shadowboxing as he awaited transfer to the Meeting Room.

Meeting Room?

Sorry.

As outlined earlier, the Rules of Challenge stipulate that the Champion of the Challenged Firm comes to the Challenging

Firm's base, den, or lair in a blindfolded state. The first person the Challengee sees after blindfold removal will be his opponent in the Fight. It is generally accepted that to avoid nasty accidents (like the time when Bruiser Jago clapped eyes on Conchita, the Bandit Queen's Chihuahua, before Deathstar McMurtrie, the true Challenger, caught Mexican rabies, and died horribly soon afterward), the meeting is rigged. The Meeting Room is a sort of cell, in which the fighters are shut up together with brown paper bags on their heads and then revealed to each other in total privacy. In the case of the *Kleptomanic,* the Meeting Room had been established in the base of funnel three. "All ready?" said the captain to Nanny Pete.

"Ready," said Nanny Pete through his gumshield.

"Beft of luck!" shouted tiny Nosy Clanger, who only reached up to his knee.

"Ta, Nosy," said Nanny Pete, polite as always. The crane hooked his harness. He went up, up, up into the spiderweb rigging and down, down, down into the funnel.

The crane hook came back empty. There was a rumble and clash of sliding doors. The ship's clock struck the hour. Silence fell, broken only by the teeny thump of Nosy Clanger's feet on the deck, for Nosy was very excited and had to be leaping continually to and fro. There was also the sound of an engine. The white van (a new, small version, mechanically even more dreadful than the previous one) arrived on the quay with a sickly clatter. Leaning over the side, Daisy saw Hilda the Builder emerge from the exhaust smoke. Hilda stood for a moment, waiting for the wobble of her outer reaches to steady. She took a pat of lard from her overall pocket and ate a few strengthening mouthfuls. Then she waved away the crane hook and started to walk up the gangway. Ten minutes later she was standing on the Jag deck, puffed and wobbling, a pool of sweat spreading round her feet. With her in her personal pond were White Van Dan, Dickie the Brickie with the traditional brown paper bag over his head, a couple of hundred of the Firm, and, in an old sack, the arms and right leg of the Royal Edward.

Daisy, standing to one side, smelled that smell of burnt carpet and old grease and ancient, ancient fags. Really, how quite unsuitable, she thought. What if a child were to see them . . . ?

She shook her head to clear it. Beside her, a small voice said, "If it waf me, I'd fpifflicate 'em."

She looked down. There at waist level was Nosy Clanger, looking ferocious. "Quite so," she said, and for a moment she did feel very, very annoyed with these horrid building people who wanted to upset these poor, nice burglars and knock down houses and cause fuss and dust and general mess.

The builders and the captain were going into the wheelhouse. During a brief but moving ceremony, the shields containing the bits of the Edward were hung on the wall so they made an exploded bear, headless.

"Even Steven," said Hilda the Builder, according to long-established usage. "I say this is a correck Challenge."

"Nice one," said the captain with all due formality. Hilda and the svelte captain returned to the Fighting Deck.

Daisy knew she should have been concentrating on the ceremony. But at that moment, out of the crowd, there leaped the face of her brother. A surge of nanny spirit rose in her. So dirty, that face, peering round the striped jersey of a stout burglar. Covered in oil, nearly as bad as a builder. She opened her mouth to give him a sound ticking off. But suddenly he was gone.

"I'd give that Dickie fuch a feeing to," said Nosy, down there.

The frustration of seeing her grubby brother was seething in her. "Oh, for goodness' *sake*," she snapped. "You're too small. And too silly. Why don't you find someone your own size? Like a smelly *mouse* or something."

Nosy's toothless mouth fell open. He seemed for a moment speechless. Then in tones of gigantic scorn, he said, "Ha!"

Daisy had never seen so many hurt feelings crammed into such a tiny person. She knew that the last shreds of nanny-ishness had led her to say something absolutely awful. She began saying she was sorry, sorry, sorry.

Too late.

The minute space Nosy had occupied was now empty,

and she was apologizing to empty air. From high above, she could hear a thin voice, crying, "Small? Small? *Small?*" and a peal of tiny but hideous laughter.

"You busted our van," said Hilda the Builder at the outdoor tea that preceded the Challenge.

"Dearie me," said the captain sweetly, pouring a cup. "Milk?"

"Five sugars," said Hilda the Builder, who was standing next to Dickie the Brickie, who had a brown paper bag over his head.

"Oi," said Dan, and there was something nervy in his bounce. "What about the fight?"

"Our boy is waiting in the Meeting Room, bless him," said the captain.

Suddenly a crane hook whizzed out of the sky. It caught in the back of Dickie's dungarees. "Ooer," said Dickie.

"Doesn't he like heights?" said the captain.

"Loves 'em," said Dan.

Dickie the Brickie nodded. He was two meters tall and a meter wide. In the pockets of his enormous dungarees he carried a couple of dozen bricks without noticing the extra weight. It was his habit, when peckish, to munch one. Even now, a dribble of red dust was filtering down his dungaree bib under the paper bag rim.

"Up he goes," said the captain.

And up went Dickie the Brickie into the cable-webbed void.

Not quite a void. Voids are empty. And a space is not empty if it contains anything at all. Even something tiny. Even something as tiny as Nosy Clanger.

There was a slithering noise above Dickie's head, as of a light weight slipping down a heavy cable. Something small but surprisingly heavy landed on Dickie's shoulder. A tiny voice hissed in his ear, "Villin!" Minute hands grasped the edge of the paper bag and ripped it in twain. Dickie the Brickie found himself gazing into the tiny tattooed features of Nosy Clanger, twisted into a grin of pure spite. "Challenge!" cried Nosy. "You will periff miferably!"

"Not as miferably as you will," said Dickie, in whose pea-sized brain a light was slowly dawning. "Oi!" he cried, directing his voice between his feet at the now-tiny deck. "I seen one!"

"Challenger!" cried White Van Dan, according to ancient ritual.

The captain looked up, shaking her head. The ritual could not be changed. The die was cast. "That is the first of us seen, and therefore let him be our challenger," she said. And Daisy, standing next to her, saw the long red nails sink into the palms of the long white hands.

Things had gone badly wrong.

Cassian had every confidence in his errand. He normally did when there was something mechanical to be dealt with.

He whizzed down the ladders to the engine room and said, "Progress report, please."

"The boys on the gate say tickety boo," said one of the stokers. "Any minute now, they said. Tide's right for the next hour."

"Check," said Cassian. He trotted along the ranks of engineers. The furnaces were glowing. The safety valves were hissing. Boilers one, two, and three were up to pressure. All that was required was for the chief to pull the great knife switch that activated numbers one, two, and three entry-valve servo motors. . . .

But this is foolishly complicated stuff, best left to Cassian. The point was that the *Kleptomanic* was ready for sea.

All he had to do was persuade the chief to throw the switch.

He made a last-minute adjustment to a pressure valve and gave a word of fatherly advice to a stoker whose trimming showed room for improvement. Then, removing his length of wood from his overall pocket, he pressed the electric bell by the control-room door.

It opened a crack. There seemed to be five chains on it. "Vot?" said the chief.

Cassian noted the whirling eyes and the hostile voice, to say nothing of the chains. But as an engineer, he had a high regard for pure logic. He had made a resolution based on the fact that the chief, at the core of his being, must feel similarly.

Engines ran by pure logic. Logic was logic and left no room for sentiment.

Which shows how much Cassian knew about people.

"Chief," he said, "it is like this. There is a Challenge going on up there for your bear—"

"Mein Edward!" cried the chief, the eyes whirling like Dutch windmills.

"—but it is in your power to prevent all this bloodshed and get your Edward back."

The eyebrows rose on the chief's moon forehead. "Ja?" he said.

"Easily," said Cassian. "You will observe from your dials that we have steam up and are in all respects ready for sea."

"So?" said the chief.

"Also, I have the dock gates ready for immediate opening, and the tide is right for a safe, nay, a dignified exit. To sum up: Your bear is here, the ship is ready, the gate is open, the tide is in our favor. Let me beg you to throw the switch so we may boldly go where—"

"Schtop!" cried the chief. His eyes had stopped whirling. They now focused on Cassian with an unnerving vibration. "I cannot. I am of the Blood Royal. A Challenge is a Challenge. Honor demands that until I receive my bear by fair and legitimate means from the vinner, I can make no svitch movements."

"So you would rather live in the mud and mend filthy diesels for White Van Dan and the Firm?"

The long chin jutted. The floppy white hand dashed a tear from the eye. "Avast, tempter!" cried the chief. The door slammed.

And that, thought Cassian, looked distressingly like that.

Well, there was much to do.

The fight ring had been built between the front two of the *Kleptomanic's* four funnels. It was a square of canvas, surrounded by a velvet-covered rope. The rope was a meter off the ground. Dickie the Brickie stepped over it without effort. Nosy walked under it without ducking. The crowd roared.

Above the ring had been installed a mighty clock, the hands set to twelve noon. In each of two opposite corners of the ring was a wooden stool. Dickie the Brickie sat down on his. Giant Luggage and Nanny Pete, who had been brought blinking out of the funnel to serve as seconds, helped Nosy up onto his. The referee, Superintendent Bent Larsen of the Freeport Constabulary, entered the ring himself. "*Good* morning, ladies and gentlemen!" he cried. "And a fine bright morning it is—"

"Move it, copper!" cried the crowd.

(And it was a crowd. Up and up it stretched, like the crater of a volcano made of people. There were burglars in masks, burglars dressed as nannies, burglars in red-and-black-striped jerseys, and of course burglars dressed as builders, or builders dressed as burglars—it was hard to tell the difference, assuming there was one.)

"Orright!" roared Superintendent Bent. "Inna red corner, Dickie the Brickie! Inna other red corner, er . . . anyone got a magnifying glass, hur, hur! Aargh!" The superintendent began to hop round the ring, screaming. For Nosy Clanger had shot out and bitten him sharply on the leg.

There was an enthusiastic rumble from the crowd; violence was always highly acceptable. Dickie the Brickie locked his salami fingers and cracked his knuckles with a sound that sent seagulls squawking from their nests in the ledges of the ship.

Watching from a porthole high above, Daisy turned to Primrose, who had just returned from the kitchen. She said, "We're in trouble."

Primrose just smiled a large, calm smile and hugged the Safes of the World cake tin she had in her arms.

"But look at the size of him!"

"You wait till he has a sip of water."

Daisy looked at her sister sideways. "Not normal water?" she said.

Primrose raised her eyebrows, sweetly innocent. "Like Nana says," she said. "What you don't know can't hurt you, dear."

Daisy snarled at her.

"Temper," said Primrose.

"And now!" roared Superintendent Bent, "as is traditional, seconds will swap water bottles, just to make sure there's no dodgy dealing."

"Oh, dear," said Primrose. "I hadn't thought of that."

"Problem?" said Daisy.

"Disaster," said Primrose. She explained.

"I'll find Cassian," said Daisy.

The water bottles were swopped. "Seconds out!" cried Superintendent Bent. "No gouging, no biting, no tactical missiles or other fire weapons. Otherwise, anything goes. Round one!"

Bing, said the bell. And high overhead, the *Kleptomanic*'s great clock began to tick.

Primrose struggled through the crowd to the clear area round the red velvet ring. She started across it. A rural burglar grabbed her arm. "Can't go there, liddle missy," he said.

"But something terrible will happen!"

"Can but 'ope," said the burglar with a happy, rustic, scar-faced grin.

"I must get in!"

"Now, lookie yur," said the rural burglar, who had specialized in twocking tractors before he had run away to ship. "I knows that you nanny folks is crool 'ard. But we is burglars and we has got standards. Because we breaks the lor for a living and before you breaks the lor, you got to know where it lies, be it the Lor of the Land or, as in this case yur, the Lor of the Jungle. If you follow."

There were nods and growls all round.

"Why don't you watch with me," said the captain, who had appeared at her side.

Up in the ring, Dickie the Brickie was lumbering in circles, trying to grasp Nosy Clanger, who was launching small but apparently painful kicks at his ankles. It was going better than Primrose had expected. Just as long as Nosy did not drink the water . . .

Primrose had worked long and hard at that water. She was proud of the result. It had henbane for illness, bat kidneys for sleepiness, eggs for sloshing, and cake for clumsiness. It was in a base of her own devising, made of river foam and fish bladders, that made it taste exactly like water, only slightly thicker. And it contained a secret delay ingredient, made from the temporal lobes of snail brains, which meant that its effects took a minute to kick in.

The clock ticked round to three minutes. Bing, went the bell. The fighters returned to their corners.

"How do you think it's going?" said the captain to Daisy, who had finished a certain mission and come alongside.

"Fine," said Daisy. Her face felt as if it was made of wood. "Can we knock over the water bottle?"

"Against the rules."

"Blast the rules!"

"Not very nanny," said the captain.

"Don't care."

"The rules are the rules," said the captain. "They have been put in place to avoid a general battle."

"In that case," said Daisy, "we are going to have to make the bits of the bear vanish."

"The rules—"

"What the eye don't see, the heart don't grieve over," said Daisy.

"Besides," said the captain. "The bits are heavily guarded."

"We've thought of that," said Primrose, clutching her cake tin.

"So be good and hope for the best. It's all we can do, Primrose, dear. Primrose?"

"She's gone," said Daisy.

And she was.

There were two nanny burglars and two builders in the wheelhouse. They were sitting on opposite sides of the chart table, glaring at each other. Behind them on the wall were the six shields that bore the bits of the bear. When the door opened, they looked round. A little girl was standing there. She was wearing a pink gingham dress, white socks, and dear little black patent-leather pumps. Her hair was yellowish blond, scraped back under a pink Alice band. And her eyes were pale blue and blinked a lot. In her hand was a Safes of the World cake tin. "Hello, Mr. Big Person," said Primrose, and gave a high giggle. "I brought you some cakes."

"Ooh," said the builders. "Thoughtful. Where you gone, ship burglars?"

"Down here under the table," said the burglars, who knew how truly dangerous she was.

The little girl took the lid off the tin. "Don't your friends want some?" she said.

"No," said a voice from under the table.

"All the more for us," said the builder.

His mate looked into the tin. It contained four delicious-looking cakes, pink, with real cream, tutti-frutti sprinkles, and chocolate icing. "Sloo," he said.

"Yeah," said his mate, grabbing with unwashed hands. "Cheers, little girl. Yum." Down went the cakes.

"That's it, then," said the builders. "Scarper, kid."

But the kid did not scarper. She stood there blinking and smiling her watery smile. She had never seen anyone eat a double dose of her Extra-Fast-Acting Sleepy Cakes before, and she wanted to see what would happen.

There was a noise like two sacks of potatoes being dropped from a height. "'Scuse me," said Primrose, stepping over the bodies. "I'll take that." She started unhooking the bear-part shields from the wall.

"Oi," said the nanny burglars nervously.

"Oh, do be quiet," said Primrose. "There's a really interesting fight outside. Why don't you have a look?"

The nannies crowded to the wheelhouse windows.

"Well, then," said Primrose, gathering up the bear bits. "Bye!"

And she slipped away.

It was busy needle time.

"Seconds out!" cried Bent, by the ring. "Round two!"

And Nosy Clanger went in.

He buzzed toward Dickie the Brickie like a hungry mosquito. Dickie tried to clap one of his hands on each of Nosy's ears. But Nosy was too quick for him. The great palms came together behind him with a sound like bricks colliding. And Nosy was through, biting Dickie sharply on the leg as he passed.

The round went on.

The second part of the round consisted of Nosy pawing at his opponent's mouth, sprinting round the ring while Dickie lumbered after him. Nosy took to ducking under the ropes, probably in the hope that Dickie would trip as he chased him. Now it was the Firm's turn to boo. Nosy's leg nips had slowed Dickie down, but not enough. Swat went his mighty fist. The wind of it blew Nosy's face out of shape, and he stumbled. The next fist hurtled toward him—

Bing, went the bell.

Nosy dropped to the ground. The fist missed.

"Phew," said a couple hundred burglars.

Nosy crawled to his corner. He picked up the water bottle.

Daisy stood frozen with horror.

He rinsed his mouth out and spat.

Daisy let out her breath.

Nosy took another swig.

"Oops," said Daisy.

Nosy swallowed.

Daisy's mouth hung open, and she forgot to breathe.

"The leg bone connected to the bum bone," sang Primrose, her sewing hand a blur. "The other leg connected to the, er." Even a bear as smart as the Royal Edward did not have actual bones, so the song was pretty useless really, and Primrose had no time for useless things, including songs.

She chewed her lower lip and stitched on the other leg. She sewed the bear's bum to the bear's tum. She sewed the arms to the torso. It was a fantastically neat job, done at the high speed she had learned while sewing nanny skirts to nursery curtains behind nanny backs in earlier life. After two and a half minutes, the Royal Edward was all there except for the head: a dumpy beige bear, moth-eaten, giving off a slight, sour smell of royal and ancient dribble.

Primrose ran for the iron ladders that plunged into the oily deeps.

"Cassian!" she cried. *"Cassian!"*

But Cassian was elsewhere, doing other stuff.

At first, the special water seemed to revive Nosy. He did a couple of press-ups and danced on the rope. But inside him, Daisy knew, the henbane, raw eggs, cake, fish bladders, river foam, and snail brains would be doing their deadly work. In precisely sixty seconds, the fight was going to take a turn for the worse.

And there was nothing anyone could do about it.

"Round three!" cried Bent.

Bing, said the bell.

The fighters leaped from their stools and headed for the middle of the ring.

Daisy could now see that the mixture was definitely working on Nosy but not, perhaps, in the way Primrose had intended. He skipped confidently across the ring. His gums were no longer bared. His eyes were fixed on the point of Dickie's square, stubbly chin. They had a weird glitter.

The crowd could definitely feel that something was going on, and they liked it. "Bop 'im!" they cried.

For a moment, Nosy stood perfectly still. Then he leaped backward, landing on the red velvet rope. The rope stretched under his boots like catapult elastic. Then it shot him through the air, fists out, straight at Dickie the Brickie. Daisy caught a glimpse of Nosy's tiny face. The eyes were closed, and it wore a blissful smile. As he hurtled toward the delivery of his killer punch, Nosy was already fast asleep.

Asleep or not, things now happened extremely fast.

Dickie had been standing there with his mouth open. As Nosy's gloves hit his chin, his teeth came together with a click. He went down flat on his back, seeing stars. Nosy landed flat on his face next to him and lay snoring peacefully.

A flicker of movement caught Daisy's eye, high up by the clock. A stocky figure with thick black hair and oily overalls was up there, carrying what looked like a petrol can: Cassian.

The crowd was going barmy. Bent scratched his chin. A double knockout was against the rules, and Bent never broke the rules, unless of course someone paid him to do it.

Dickie's eyelids fluttered. He groaned, pushing himself onto one knee. The sweat of relief poured down Bent's forehead. Dickie got up and leaned on the ropes. *"One!"* cried Bent.

High among the cogs of the clock, Cassian poured the last drops from his tin into the giant springs and balance wheels. It was a blackish, gooey liquid. Where it touched the metal surfaces, it made strings, like chewing gum or extra-sticky toffee (both of which were in the mixture). A weird groaning was coming from the machinery as the treacly goo spread through it. You would have said the cogs were moving more slowly.

You would have been right.

Cassian threw the tin into the works and slid down a funnel stay toward a dark hatch leading into the bowels of the ship.

There was much to do and little time.

Primrose marched across the engine-room floor, clutching the Royal Edward to her pink gingham chest. It seemed hotter than usual down here, with more steam, and bigger mechanical thumpings, and hollower clangings. She clutched the Royal Edward more tightly—even headless, he was a comforting bear. Kitchens were fine, but she was not so sure about engine rooms.

Too late to worry now.

She was at the door of the control room. Cassian had told her about the bell push. Using the paw of the Royal Edward, she gave the bell a prod.

"*Nooo!*" cried the voice from within. A pair of whirling brown eyes appeared in the holes in the glass. Primrose held up the bear.

There was a moment of silence, as far as silence was possible in the engine room. Then: "*Yeeees!*" cried the voice from within. There was the sound of five chains coming off, a dozen locks unlocking. The chief stood there, jaw swinging, getting ready to say something fantastically stupid.

Primrose got in first. "Listen up, you big palooka," she said. "This is your bear, but as even you should be able to see, it has got a bit of a head shortage. And I cannot tell a lie: we nicked the bits we didn't have. But of course it is your bear and has been all along, so in my view this whole Challenge business is just a load of nonsense. I'll put it back if you want to be all silly and royal and sporting. Or I can sew it back together good as new with my busy needle. And then we can forget about this Challenge nonsense and you can do what our Cassian wants. Right?"

The chief fiddled with his fingers, racked between love and duty. "Smellink so good," he mumbled. "Rules is rules, but schtolen from me by rewolution men and poor sing, no head. *In ewent of emergency, brek gless!*" Picking up a hammer, he took a mighty swing at the glass case containing, under its gilt wrought-iron crown and eagle, the head of the Royal Edward.

Glass flew everywhere. The head rolled free. Primrose scooped it up. "Moment," she said, one eye screwed up, threading her needle against an arc lamp.

It was done in a trice.

"There you go," said Primrose, tossing the chief his bear.

"Not to throw poor him!" snapped the chief. Then the tidal wave of emotion smote him.

Reader, it was a fearful sight. That enormous man in blue and gold kissed his teddy. He hugged it. He sniffed it, drooled on it, and hugged it a bit more. Primrose was forced to look away.

And saw Cassian, one eyebrow up on his oily forehead, wearing an expression of bright hope and expectation—

"Nooooo!" bellowed the chief. "*Nodings happen!*"

"I beg your—"

"*I am pressink tummy,*" howled the chief, pressing it. "*My algernon is supposed to say, 'Good evenink, your royal highness, I vish you many codfish and absolutely no volca-noes.'* But I *press* and I *press* and *nodings* I get. Not a *sprat.* Not a *geyser*—"

"Oops," said Primrose. "Wrong bear." And before the chief knew what was happening, she had twitched the moldering beast out of Prince Beowulf's hands and darted into the coal heaps.

"What's wrong?" said Cassian. "We haven't got much time."

"Hold it," said Primrose. "I need to talk to Daisy. Stay by the ventilator."

"But—"

But Primrose was gone.

15

The clock's second hand seemed to be moving too slowly. Am I going crazy? thought Bent Larsen, the referee. During the first second of the count, he took a cheese sandwich from his pocket and ate it. Slowly. He said, "I don't believe that clock."

"Ship's time is ship's time," said the captain's voice, elegant but nautical. Another voice said from the crowd, *"Do we believe in the ship's clock?"*

"Yeeees!" roared many voices.

"Then count!"

"Two!" roared the crowd. Bent ate the other half of his sandwich, even more slowly than the first, while weird groanings came from the clock. *". . . and . . . Three!"*

Another long pause. "Next time, louder!" cried a voice. Daisy's voice. Nosy needed to be woken up, and a good shout might do it.

"*F—*" hissed the crowd.

"Not yet!" cried Daisy. Cassian had overdone the clock goo. A huge syrupy strand was hanging from the hour hand. Hilda the Builder's moon face and button nose turned up at it, frowning.

"*—our!*" cried the crowd as the second hand crawled round.

"*Fixx!*" cried Hilda.

"Gerroff!" cried the crowd. "Gerraway!" There was a general soup of roaring. Fights broke out. Someone fried an egg and ate it.

"*Five!*"

"Up, Nosy!" cried Daisy. "Up!"

But it was not Nosy who was up. It was White Van Dan, swinging skyward like an awful ape on one of the taut hawsers supporting the funnel, heading for the clock. The crowd watched him, mouths open. The strand of goo from the clock stretched like chewing gum and fell into the gigantic mouth of Hilda the Builder. "Treacle!" cried Hilda, slobbering delightedly. "Yummmmmmmmmmm!" And could say no more, because the go-slow goo had got its deadly grip on her jaws and stuck them together sure as superglue.

High above, Dan had reached the clock. He scooped a sample of goo into his tobacco tin, got some on his hand, and wiped his nose on the back of it.

"*Six!*" cried Bent Larsen and chorus, far below him.

"*Fix!*" yelled Dan, or meant to. But the goo had spread from the back of his hand to his nose and from his nose to his lips, so the sound came out, "*Fxxxxxxx,*" like an escape of steam. He hung there, lips sealed, gibbering.

"He looks," said Daisy, "like a sloth."

"Only slower," said the captain. "Goodness." Her ruby lips were pressed together, her knuckles the color of ivory. "If he can claim the fix, with evidence, before the end of the countdown, he automatically wins. There will be a debate over ship's time, of course, but—"

"Nosy blinked!" cried Daisy. "He definitely blinked!"

And indeed, there on the canvas, the tiny shell-like eyelids of Nosy Clanger had moved.

"Not long till he wakes up," said Daisy.

The captain sighed. "But then what?" she said.

High on his wire, White Van Dan was hard at work. His lips were still sealed. But he had taken from his dungarees pocket a small pointing trowel. With this tool he had scraped go-slow goo from his baccy tin and smeared it on his boots. Then he stood up on the hawser and let himself fall forward until he was hanging head downward, directly above the ring. The crowd gasped. Very slowly, White Van Dan descended on twin strings of goo toward the tiny figure sprawled on the canvas. And all the time, he was doing something with his thick, tattooed hands.

Someone was tugging at Daisy's sleeve. "Oi!" hissed a voice. Primrose's voice.

"What?" said Daisy impatiently.

"The bear's squeak," said Primrose.

"What are you talking about?"

"It's missing. It used to be in its tum. It isn't anymore."

"Oh," said Daisy, and thrust her hands into the pockets of her nanny coat, the better to think.

Her hand met something metallic and drum shaped. She pulled it out, frowning. It looked like a miniature concertina. It could almost have been a weird, elaborate, massively overcomplicated—(She remembered something falling on the Roller's floor; falling from the torso, in fact; picking it up, putting it in her pocket . . . from the torso.)—bear's squeak or voice box. She gave it to Primrose.

"Ahem," said Primrose. "Captain?"

"What?"

"I need a burglar who can throw."

"Of course, of course," said the captain distractedly.

"Bruce used to play cricket for Australia. Expert at stealing runs. Bruce!"

Bruce came over. Primrose gave him his instructions. Bruce scratched his head. "That ventilator?" he said, pointing.

"That ventilator."

Bruce took the voice box of the Royal Edward, wound it up, and threw. The little silver drum soared into the air, went dead center into the red mouth of the ventilator, and disappeared from view.

"*Seven!*" roared the crowd.

"*Seven!*" said the ventilator pipe far below. Cassian looked up. There was a rattle and a clatter. And out of the ventilator pipe there clattered a small silver drum.

Cassian caught it before it could hit the deck, stuffed it into a slot he had cut in the bear's middle, and ran across to the control room. He held up the bear. The chief's eyes whirled. Cassian pressed the bear's stomach. "*Good evenink, your royal highness,*" said the bear. "*I vish you—*"

The door crashed open. Loving hands snatched the Royal Edward. "*Velcome home!*" cried the chief, embracing his old pal.

"And now," said Cassian, "your side of the bargain."

"What's he doing?" said Primrose.

"Dread to think," said the captain, as if she already had thought and did not like it.

"What's that?" said Daisy.

Everyone suddenly stood very still. For a second, a hush fell.

For deep, deep under the steel deck on which they stood, something had moved. It might have been a tiny earthquake or a door slamming far away in a house.

Then it stopped, as if it had never been.

"Just settling," said the captain. She really was very, very pale. "By the way, where's your brother?"

Daisy found it easy to like the captain. Which was odd, because Daisy did not like anyone much except her brother and sister. It was a most peculiar feeling. Because she was not used to it, it took the form of worrying about all the work that would go on, the misery and suffering that would result if the poor kind nanny burglars had to leave their ship or got arrested or something because of a Challenge that had gone wrong. . . .

Goodness, thought Daisy, who thanks to years of nannies was used to taking the blame. It is practically my fault.

She found she was holding the captain's hand and the captain was holding hers back.

"*Eight!*" roared Bent Larsen.

Up there on the canvas, Nosy Clanger rose on one tiny knee.

"Ooh!" cried the crowd.

Nosy fell down again.

"Ah!" cried the crowd.

Far below, in the *Kleptomanic*'s engine room, Cassian stood at a huge console gleaming with polished brass. Around him stood his handpicked henchmen, all of them with high mechanical qualifications—safecrackers, train robbers, bank vault tunnelers. Beside him beamed Chief Engineer Crown Prince Beowulf of Iceland, the Royal Edward in his arms.

"Report," said Cassian into the speaking tube at his ear.

"Water levels equal, guv," said a voice.

For Cassian, this was the culmination of much work. Naturally he knew all about liners, having read the Arthur Mee *Books of Knowledge* from *C* to shining *Z* (*A* and *B* had been destroyed in an experiment).

This is his master list:

1. Oil everything.
2. Trim bunkers, specially number nine, redistributing contents in nos. two, three, four, and seven for optimum stability (port bunkers odd, starboard bunkers even).
3. Check speaking tubes.
4. Check oil, water, other fuels, generators, food, sheets, blankets, lifeboats, butter, cheese, and all ancillary machinery.
5. Check speaking tubes again, also engine-room telegraphs.
6. Check lock gates.

7. Light boilers.
8. Persuade chief engineer to throw master switch.
9. That's it.

All those years, the *Kleptomanic* had been sitting in a dock—a huge basin of water with a gate at one end, so no matter whether the tide was high or low outside, inside it would always be at the same level. This morning, Cassian had sent his dock gang out on to the sluice gates to open the hatches that would make the water level inside the dock the same as the water level outside. Stealthily, the levels had equalized, and the gates had swung open in a sullen swirl of black water, leaving the *Kleptomanic* pointing at the open creek.

After the restoration of the Edward, Cassian had gone to the console. "Mornin', Fingers," he said.

"Mornin', Chief."

"Steam up?"

"Steam up."

Earlier that morning, he had given the order to get up steam. From nooks and crannies and black beds in the bunkers the stokers had poured—gold diggers, grave robbers, treasure hunters, and other low forms of criminal life, good for nothing but shovel work. A couple of arsonists had got sticks and paper going in the cavernous hearths. Then the coal started to rain down, caught, glowed, and the heat rushed round the boiler tubes and the water boiled and turned to steam and waited behind its valves to push up the huge pistons linked to the shafts that plunged through the ship's back end and turned the five-meter bronze propellers that had once driven the ship across the Atlantic in a breathtaking six days.

Now, two hours later, the needles on the pressure dials were crawling up to the red line.

Cassian uncapped a speaking tube. "Report," he said.

One of the tubes was saying, with several hundred voices, *"Fiixxx!"* Another, the one Cassian was listening to, said, "Gates open, guv. Ready when you are."

"Check," said Cassian. "Test drive train."

"All systems nominal, guv," said Fingers.

"Bridge?" said Cassian into a speaking tube.

"All present and correck."

"Same here."

"Dead slow astern, then," said the bridge.

"Fiixxxxx," roared the faraway crowd.

Ding, went the telegraph.

Steam whooshed into the cylinder. The gleaming cams shifted. The great shaft turned and kept turning.

And all the time, White Van Dan was descending on his slow ropes of goo. Now the people below could see what he was doing. He had pulled the pencil from behind his ear. Fighting goo at every letter, he was writing on the slab of four-by-two that he always carried in the back pocket of his filthy, low-slung jeans. Below him, the ring was a white square, Dickie the Brickie in his corner, dribbling brick dust down his fearful jaw as he snacked, Bent Larsen stooped over the tiny flat-out figure of Nosy Clanger, whose eyes were once more closed.

Whose eyes were suddenly open.

The eyes looked straight up, the whites showing all the way round the irises. They focused straightaway on descending Dan. Bent Larsen, following his gaze, looked up.

And saw, in reverse order, this: the clock, the string of goo, White Van Dan, and the length of four-by-two in Dan's hand. And on the four-by-two, words, scribbled in huge ignorant writing: FIX. OFISHUL PROTETS.

Give or take a bit of spelling, it was the correct formula.

"Stop the fight!" roared Bent.

The *Kleptomanic* moved again.

This time, it did not stop.

The crowd stilled. A cloud of gulls rose from the upperworks. They were already nervous from all the shouting, and now they wheeled and shrieked and watched with their mad yellow eyes as something the size of a city block slid ponderously from between the piers and warehouses. It sailed, bright white against the blue as it stopped going backward and started going forward, pointing its nose out of the long black creek toward the sea.

The gulls thought about going to sit on the ship again. They soared among the black plumes billowing from the funnels, nervous, not quite liking to perch.

A gull's life is hard and uncertain. Gulls get good at smelling out trouble before it happens.

16

Hilda the Builder had just managed to wrench her huge lips apart, using both hands. "Oi!" she cried in a voice still goo-muffled. She began puffing and wobbling through the crowd toward the captain. "Dickie!" she yelled over her bloated shoulder. "Get Dan!"

Dickie the Brickie reached up, grabbed White Van Dan, and hauled him down into the fight ring. Dan took his boots off. The smell floated across to Nosy, who sat up suddenly. "Have I won?" he said.

Dan shook his head, lips still stuck.

"Oh," said Nosy, disappointed. "Phwoar. Your feet fmell awful."

Dickie the Brickie produced a nasty grinding sound.

"Cheeky," he said, blowing a cloud of brick dust. "Pygmy boy."

Things then began to happen fast. Nosy, refreshed by his short sleep and still sensitive about his height, bit Dickie on the leg. Dickie picked up Nosy, swung him twice round his head, and threw him into the sea.

Nosey cried, "I can't fwiiiiiii—" The word ended in a small white splash in the broad black creek.

"Oi!" cried Bent Larsen, blowing his ref's whistle. But the sound was drowned in a great roar of burglarious rage as AAA Aardvark Child Minding and Security fell on the Firm.

"Oi, sunshine, your boy is well out of order," said the captain to White Van Dan in fluent Criminal. "It was a fair cop. There was a fix, granted, which I hereby admit as per the rules, clause 14, section Q (i). But we have, as it now appears, got the Edward. And possession being nine points of the law, plus it was the chief engineer's bear anyway, what you going to do about it?"

White Van Dan's face was hard as cement. He made no answer.

"Can you, frinstance, drive a ship?" said the captain. "It means turning up on time and not stopping for tea every ten minutes."

"Fine," said Dan. "See what you mean. You win." His face now looked like cement in a mixer, sloshed around by strong paddles of emotion. "But wot am I gunna tell the boys? And Hilda?"

"We keep the chief. You wouldn't like him. Or Iceland. If anyone asks, you have won, and I shall give you a certificate. We are off, under clause 28, section B, viz. in the event of a fix, the fixer will leave the manor, no error. There is no call for nastiness or unpleasantness. We shall put you ashore in one of the lifeboats."

"Fair doos," said White Van Dan.

"Daisy," said the captain over her shoulder. "Could you ask Cassian to arrange this?"

Silence, except for the earsplitting roar of fighting burglars.

"Daisy?"

But Daisy seemed to have vanished.

Then a small, clear voice shouted, "Over there!"

It cut through the roar like a knife, that voice. For a moment the world hushed. The moment spread, became a second, then a minute. All eyes were directed over the side.

This is what they saw.

They saw Daisy, now wearing shorts and a T-shirt, loping with a ballerina's grace to the far outside end of the *Kleptomanic*'s bridge, where it hung over the water like a diving board. They saw her arms go forward, out, forward again. And as they went forward for the last time, she launched herself into space, arms outstretched, body arched back in a perfect swallow dive, down, down, down, until she entered the creek with the smallest feather of a splash.

There was a rattle of applause. *"Neuf points!"* cried the captain.

"Do what?" said White Van Dan.

"Shut it and get in the lifeboat, concrete features," said Pete Fryer, who was standing close at hand.

"Manners!" said Dan sniffily. He had never had a nanny, so no one had ever in his long life of crime spoken to him in that tone of voice.

But he went down the ladder and squeezed into the lifeboat next to Hilda the Builder. Dan had made a decision. He would stop all this building nonsense and go into the security trade. There would be uniforms, of course: suits with gold badges, truncheons instead of hammers. They would get paid for hanging around drinking tea near banks and jewelers. Pickings in the security industry would be astonishingly rich.

The future looked bright.

Daisy went down and down, until the waters of the creek were as black as the blackest midnight. She was not worried, though. She was thinking how upset poor Nosy must be, floundering tinily after all that brilliant fighting. It was as if something ancient and powerful was driving her on. Nosy felt like part of her family.

Part of her *what?*

Deep under the surface of the creek, she was suddenly

very confused. She had been looked after by nannies for so long that the idea of families was strange and distant. Now, weirdly, it made her think of the captain, and of course her dear brother and sister, with somewhere in the background, small and wobbly, Papa Darling. . . .

Here she stopped thinking. Because far above, in a twinkle of white water, she saw two of the smallest legs in the world, kicking.

Kicking frenziedly to keep their owner afloat.

And failing.

Daisy whooshed up to the surface and took a deep breath. The *Kleptomanic* rose above her like a cliff. Builders who had failed to get places in Dickie and Hilda's lifeboat were falling down the side like fruit off a tree. Eyeing them with a diver's scorn, she turned away, looking for Nosy. The water slopped black and empty and cold.

Ten meters away from her, bubbles rose.

She dived after them.

The line of bubbles rose silvery and wobbling, pointing at a tiny white frog drifting down, down toward the mud and old fridges of the creek bottom. A frog wearing huge boxing shorts. Nosy.

Daisy had never done any lifesaving before. But she knew exactly what to do. She kicked firmly downward, grabbed the frog by its shorts, and headed for the surface. Her head broke water. "Help!" she cried.

And from all along the rail of the *Kleptomanic* there rolled a long, delighted cheer.

It was pretty straightforward after that. A rubber dinghy with Pete Fryer at the helm picked them up. Held upside down, Nosy gurgled forth a great deal of water and started snoring. Many builders passed, vacating the ship as per agreement with the captain, heading for shore in lifeboats and making gestures of the rudest type. Daisy put her nose in the air. "Sticks and stones may break my bones, but signs will never hurt me," she said.

"Quite fo," said Nosy, opening his eyes.

"You're better!" cried Daisy, pink with delight.

"I had him right where I wanted him," said Nosy. "I waf robbed."

Then they were alongside, and the crane was coming down, and up they soared to the Jag deck, where the captain was waiting with Primrose and Cassian. "Darlings!" said the captain.

"It waf nuffink," said Nosy, beaming modestly from knee level and not noticing that he was by no means the center of attention. Red Crook burglars hustled him away to the sick bay. The captain smiled sweetly at the departing stretcher and pulled out a telescope.

The creek was much wider now. The *Kleptomanic* was heading straight for the open sea. "Steady as she goes," said the captain. "Now, Daisy. I want a word. Ah, well done, children." For Cassian had brought up a giant fluffy towel from the First-Class Airing Hall, and Primrose had whipped Daisy up a large, dark cocoa strong enough to blot out the taste of the creek.

"A good job well done," said the captain. "I had no idea you were such a splendid lifesaver."

"Nor me," said Daisy. The creek had washed away the last traces of nanny attitude. Now she was grinning in the modest way she had seen girls grin in the *Nice Big Book for Girls*. "It's in the blood, I suppose."

"The blood?"

"I don't know if you've ever heard of Grace Darling?" said Daisy. "Daughter of the keeper of the Longstone Light. On a hideous stormy day she rowed out with her dad and rescued a lot of people from the sea in Scotland. Her dad was my great-great-great-grandpa. So I suppose you could say it was in the blood—are you all right?"

For the captain had gone white as a gull's stomach and was swaying on her ten-centimeter heels. She said, in a strange, breathy voice, "So what's your name?"

"Darling."

There was a silence. Then Daisy said, "Timberrrrrr!" And Cassian and Primrose, practiced in teamwork after years of nanny torture, stepped behind the captain and caught her just as she went down like a tree, spark out.

"Uh?" said Cassian.

"I've got a funny feeling about this," said Primrose.

So had Daisy.

Daisy was looking at her brother and sister, one on either side of the captain's pale, unconscious face, so there were three faces in a line.

Give or take a bit of age and makeup, the three faces were alike. Three peas in a pod was the expression that came to mind.

"Bring her round," said Daisy grimly.

They poured a bucket of water over the captain. The eyes opened. They did not look sleepy. In fact, Daisy thought, they looked as if she had been faking, to give herself time to think about what she was going to say.

But when the eyes settled on the children, they filled up with tears.

"Oi," said Daisy. "Was there something you wanted to tell us?"

"Don't," said softhearted Primrose, holding the captain's hand. "Not till she's had some eggnog or something."

"Wha—?" said Cassian.

"Idiot!" said his sisters. "Don't you understand *anything*?"

Cassian scowled. "What is it?" he said.

"Curiosity killed the cat," said Daisy.

"Question and answer is no substitute for conversation," said Primrose.

"'Scuse me," said Fingers, chief stoker, "but we've got a

bearing running hot on number-two shaft, and chief says he's busy talking to his bear."

"Coming," said Cassian. He went.

"Are you sure?" said the captain to the two sisters when their brother had left.

"As eggs is eggs."

"But—"

Both sisters sniffed.

The captain fell silent.

None of them noticed they were all holding hands.

It was a tough three weeks.

Cassian was awake at all hours, supervising the engines as they screwed the ship ever south and west. Having moved his mattress to a warm corner of the stokehold, he made it absolutely clear that he did not want to talk to any girls about anything, not even if it was extremely important. So naturally his sisters let him stew in his own juice.

As the weather got hotter, Primrose found the chef, used to chillier northern climes, sitting tomato-faced in a pool of sweat by his ranges. So she took over the kitchens. Sea air makes people hungry. The burglars were organized into two teams or watches (the breaking watch and the entering watch) because a ship never stops, day or night, so there must always be someone awake, even if it is only to bring flying fish downstairs for frying. And if someone is awake, someone is hungry. So if it is not huge lunches, it is midnight feasts. It never stops, and nor did Primrose.

As for Daisy, she spent a lot of time talking to the captain.

On the twenty-second day, Nosy Clanger, who because of his extreme lightness could get farther up the mast than anyone else, cried, "I fee land!"

Nobody paid any attention. Nosy had said the same thing three times a day for two weeks, having decided after his near drowning that he was a salty son of the sea who could see a black dog in a coal cellar from outside. But if you keep on saying the same thing often enough, sooner or later you will be right. And on this day, half an hour later, a small, palm-fringed shore did indeed loom above the horizon. Not long after that, the *Kleptomanic* glided through the entrance to a lagoon, and her anchors roared down into water as clear and bright as emeralds.

"Finished with engines," said Cassian, who was on the bridge. "Good grief. What's that?"

The *Kleptomanic* lay deep in a horseshoe of white beach. Behind the beach was thick tropical forest, from which rose a slim thread of smoke, perhaps from a campfire. On the beach, hopping up and down and waving at the city-block-sized ship lying rusty black in the lagoon, was a man. A large man, dressed in rags. Rags that might once, in another life, have been gents' formal evening wear. Except that now the bow tie was tied round the head to keep the filthy hair out of the crusty eyes, and the sleeves had been hacked off the jacket, whose pockets were now full of wild bananas, and the trousers ended just below the scabby knees.

Cassian focused the telescope. "Goodness me!" he cried. "It's Papa!"

Daisy cleared her throat nervously. "Yes," she said. She took the captain by the hand. "And this," she said, "is our own dear, true mama."

"Who is *so* proud of you," said the captain.

This time it was Cassian who fainted.

17

At this point in the average book, the author dips his pen elbow deep in the old golden syrup, and there are a couple of pages of tears and laughter, after which all and sundry live happily ever after, except the bad guys, who lose limbs.

It was not like that on the *Kleptomanic*. Not quite, anyway. In fact, Papa Darling and the captain sat on opposite sides of the chart table and seemed to be having some trouble thinking of things to say to each other. Cassian, having received a bucket of seawater in the face from his unsympathetic sisters, sat groggily on the floor with his back against the wall. "Out," said Daisy. She and Primrose dragged him by the legs onto the Jag deck.

"Away," said Daisy, shooing off Giant Luggage and a gaggle

of emotional burglars who were staring in at the bridge windows, hankies at the ready.

The Caribbean air soon brought Cassian back to his full wits. "How come she didn't know it was us earlier?" he said.

"Secretary Mummy changed our names to make us sound richer. We're really called Jane, Mary, and John. And Papa moved house to Avenue Marshal Posh after Captain Mummy left, and it was Secretary Mummy who lost her temper and ripped up the bear and brought the bum back."

"Silly fool," said Primrose. "By the way, we're not changing back."

"Hardly worth it," said Cassian. "So what now?"

"They thrash it out."

"What?"

"It. Us. Life. All that. I think." They were walking down toward the engine room now. There was a silence, broken only by the clatter of shoes on iron ladders. "None of our business," said Daisy.

"Yes, it is," said Cassian.

"No, it—"

They had arrived at the chief engineer's console. "Listen," said Cassian. "Even burglars are interested in this kind of man and woman and children stuff. So there's no reason why we shouldn't be either."

"Yes, there is."

"Why?"

Silence.

"Why?" said Cassian.

"Because Nanny says so," said Primrose.

Silence. A long, horrid silence. "But we never pay a blind bit of notice to anything Nanny says," said Daisy.

"Yep," said her brother and sister.

"So."

Cassian took the lid off the voice pipe marked BRIDGE. A voice floated into the hum of the engine room. Papa Darling's voice.

"Well?" he was saying. "Where did you go to, all those years ago?"

"I left."

"I am acquainted with the central dynamic of your thesis," said Papa Darling.

"And on what date did I leave?"

"You will kindly refrain from using judgmental speech patterns with regard to myself."

"Allow me to remind you, Papa Darling," said the captain's voice, "that I have rescued you and that at any moment I could unrescue you, with the assistance of my two hundred loyal burglars, trained in violence, larceny, and nanny skills."

There was a silence, in which the children could practically hear Papa go pale.

"So. On what date did I leave?"

"Ninth of August. Ten years ago."

"Wrong."

"But I wrote it down in my diary."

"It was the seventeenth of July. It took you three weeks to notice."

"What?"

"Our life together. You got up in the morning, read the newspaper at breakfast, went to the office, got back at eight if you got back at all, nodded a lot at dinner, made transatlantic telephone calls till midnight, and went to bed. Every day, weekends included, except when you were on a business trip. You never seemed to notice whether I was there or not, and you always insisted on those ghastly nannies. So one day I was watching the horse racing on the wide-screen TV, you know, the one you gave me to shut me up, and a chap came in, black mask, striped jersey, bag marked SWAG. He said he was a burglar, poor simp, as if I hadn't guessed. And of course he was absolutely hopeless at it. So my heart went out to him, really. I mean I was a bit short of people to look after, and he was so useless. So I helped him with the burglary and he introduced me to all these diamond geezers and we found the ship and I started the agency and looked after him and his friends, and you may say it is wrong to burgle, but if you have got a nanny agency full of burglars, it makes sure that you only burgle people who are big enough idiots to use nanny agencies, and most of them deserve it."

"Tosh," said Papa. "You done a runner, with a thief."

"Talking about thieves," said the captain, "what exactly is it you do at Darling Gigantic?"

"Property development. Enhancement of land values by subdivision and the creation of dwelling units."

The captain sighed. "Translate into English, if you please."

"Buying land—"

"Nature reserves."

"Sometimes."

"And building millions of cheap and nasty houses on them."

"People gotta live somewhere."

"Strikes me," said the captain, "that you are a large-scale thief yourself and that you do your nicking from people who are not all that rich in the first place."

"Wouldn't know," said Papa, and now there was definitely a sulky note in his voice.

"Kev," said the captain, "you know this to be true."

"Don't call me Kev," yelped Papa Darling. "Nobody knows I'm called Kev. In the business, they call me Colin."

"But you're not in the business anymore," said the captain sweetly. "That secretary woman with the jewels has got all the loot. She made sure of that when she left you here. Didn't she?"

"Yep," said Papa Darling, in a tired voice the children had never heard before. "It's true. By gum, you're still a fine-looking woman, Queenie. But don't call me Kev, all right?"

"We'll see," said the captain. "By the way, you don't look so bad yourself. Bit porky, mind. But if we put you on first-floor drainpipe and fire escape training for a month or two, that'll sort itself out."

There was a pause. Then Papa Darling said, "Thanks, Queenie."

"Don't thank me," said the captain. "Thank the people who made it happen."

"Who?"

"The children. Brilliantly trained in violence, cookery, engineering, and sabotage."

"Stone me," said Papa, right out of his depth.

"They saved my ship," said the captain. "They are a credit to their parents. And now their parents must show them love."

"Does this mean," said Papa, sounding hopeful, "that you and me might, you know, get back together again? Because I'm up for it if you are—"

"As far as I am concerned, Colin," said the captain, and even via the voice pipe the children heard Papa wince, "you are just another first-year, first-story man, on extra lav-cleaning duties. Other than that, we shall see."

Then there was silence.

Cassian and Primrose stared at Daisy in horror. "Love?" they said.

"Grim, I grant you," said Daisy. "But I have a feeling that things are going to get better."

"Hmm," said her brother and sister. Both of them could feel, however, that there was indeed a strange optimism in the air.

They sat for a while in silence. It was indeed most puzzling. Then Primrose said, "What's that?"

For from another of the speaking tubes there suddenly came the sound of music.

"The ballroom," said Cassian.

"Come on," said Daisy.

They went.

Okay. Golden-syrup time.

The gallery of the ballroom was thronged with burglars, some of them sobbing openly into hankies. They were watching the dance floor.

By the side of the floor stood the huge grand piano. A woman in a red velvet ball gown was playing it. The tune was "Stand by Me." A man was singing the song: a man wearing the tattered shreds of formal evening wear. The woman was the captain. The man was Papa Darling, obliging with a few bars of the old favorite before reporting for bog-cleaning duty.

Pete Fryer was standing next to the children. "Ah," he said, with a catch in his voice. "In't it Rolls?"

"I beg your pardon?"

"Rolls-Royce, choice."

The children made no reply. They had the impression that if he had closed his eyes, tears would have rolled out. And those eyes seemed completely attached to the captain. Daisy understood. A skilled and charming burglar like Pete could not spend so much time so close to a clever, elegant criminal mastermind like the captain without an attachment developing. She sighed. She said, "The saddest words, Nanny Pete: 'What might have been.'"

"Huh?" said Cassian. "Wha?"

"Poor baby," said Primrose, squeezing Pete's hand.

"Cor stone me, strike a light, what on earth are you going on about I do not know; a load of old cobblers, I am sure," said Pete, not at all convincingly. "Well, the Caribbean, eh? Nice warm place to go robbin' of an evening, or so I hear. Eh? What? Don't you think?"

"And close to America," said Daisy, to help Pete recover his composure. "There are many openings in America, one hears."

"Well, we'll be through 'em, doesn't matter what floor they're on," said Pete, drying his eyes and laughing heartily. "Well, love is love and cannot be denied, but now it is time for my pint of stout."

And the *Kleptomanic* surged on under the fiery tropical sky, carrying the Darling family—parents, children, and nanny burglars—toward Miami, Florida, home of millionaires.

Stay in your beds, little Darlings,
don't wander about in the night,
for millions of 'orrible villains
is waiting to give you a fright.
You may fink that you're sleeping in safety,
wiv all of your toys shut up tight,
but millions and millions of villains
will be there if you turn on the light.
Ohhhhhhhhhhhhh . . .
you may chain up your cycles
and lock up your fings,
but they'll bite off your fingers
and 'alf-inch your rings—